RESCUING THE LADY OF SEDGEWORTH

The Ladies of the Keep, Book Three

(Connected to The Lords of Vice Series and The Duke's Guard Series)

C.H. Admirand

© Copyright 2023 by C.H. Admirand
Text by C.H. Admirand
Cover by Dar Albert

Dragonblade Publishing, Inc. is an imprint of Kathryn Le Veque Novels, Inc.
P.O. Box 23
Moreno Valley, CA 92556
ceo@dragonbladepublishing.com

Produced in the United States of America

Revised Edition November 2024
Previous Editions/Versions Published as A Scot's Honor: 2018, 2014 & 2007 Trade Paperback Edition

Reproduction of any kind except where it pertains to short quotes in relation to advertising or promotion is strictly prohibited.

All Rights Reserved.

The characters and events portrayed in this book are fictitious. Any similarity to real persons, living or dead, is purely coincidental and not intended by the author.

ARE YOU SIGNED UP FOR DRAGONBLADE'S BLOG?

You'll get the latest news and information on exclusive giveaways, exclusive excerpts, coming releases, sales, free books, cover reveals and more.

Check out our complete list of authors, too!

No spam, no junk. That's a promise!

Sign Up Here

www.dragonbladepublishing.com

Dearest Reader;

Thank you for your support of a small press. At Dragonblade Publishing, we strive to bring you the highest quality Historical Romance from some of the best authors in the business. Without your support, there is no 'us', so we sincerely hope you adore these stories and find some new favorite authors along the way.

Happy Reading!

CEO, Dragonblade Publishing

Additional Dragonblade books by Author C.H. Admirand

The Ladies of the Keep Series
Liberating the Lady of Loughmoe (Book 1)
Bargaining with the Lady of Merewood (Book 2)
Rescuing the Lady of Sedgeworth (Book 3)

The Duke's Guard Series
The Duke's Sword (Book 1)
The Duke's Protector (Book 2)
The Duke's Shield (Book 3)
The Duke's Dragoon (Book 4)
The Duke's Hammer (Book 5)
The Duke's Defender (Book 6)
The Duke's Saber (Book 7)
The Duke's Enforcer (Book 8)
The Duke's Mercenary (Book 9)
The Duke's Rapier (Book 10)

The Lords of Vice Series
Mending the Duke's Pride (Book 1)
Avoiding the Earl's Lust (Book 2)
Tempering the Viscount's Envy (Book 3)
Redirecting the Baron's Greed (Book 4)
His Vow to Keep (Novella)
The Merry Wife of Wyndmere (Novella)

The Lyon's Den Series
Rescued by the Lyon
Captivated by the Lyon
The Lyon's Saving Grace

Historical Cookbook
Dragonblade's Historical Recipe Cookbook:
Recipes from some of your favorite Historical Romance Authors

Dedication

This book is dedicated to Kathryn Le Veque, CEO of Dragonblade Publishing, Inc., author extraordinaire, and friend. You gave me a reason to carry on when my life fell apart and helped me keep my promise to my Heavenly Hubby to finish the Lords of Vice series and continue to promote my books.

I will be forever grateful for your compassion, understanding, and a place within the Dragonblade Family. You helped me to find a purpose in my life again, and a place where I can imbue my hardheaded Dragonblade heroes with some of DJ's best qualities: his honesty, his integrity, his compassion for others, and his killer broad shoulders—and introduce them to my feisty Dragonblade heroines. Thank you!

PROLOGUE

1073 Northumbria...

GENVIEVE DE CHAURET was surprised to see two of her mother's private guards riding toward her and her father's escort from London. As they approached, a deep sense of foreboding swept up from the soles of her feet, slicing through her heart, as the first arrow hit its target between the eyes of the guard to her right.

Her father's escort had spread out to provide a wider circle of protection around her. Too late they realized their mistake, as the knight on her left met with the same fate—an arrow piercing his brain. Father's men raced toward her, but her mother's faithful guard had already reached her side.

Dupres plucked her from her horse and slammed her onto his lap as they rode away at a demonic pace amidst a hail of arrows.

Once they were well away from her father's men, Genvieve asked, "Dupres, what is the meaning of this?"

"Your mother feared your father's escort was delivering you into the hands of the enemy."

An icy ball of fear nearly stopped her breath, but she conquered it to say, "Augustin is my cousin. I have nothing to fear from him. I have missed spending time with his daughter when Angelique was in London. I look forward to a lengthy visit."

"Your cousin has betrayed his people by marrying a Saxon," the other knight spat out.

"But—"

"We are almost there," Dupres said. "It will all be clear to you in a moment."

They veered off the road into a heavily wooded area, riding deeper into the forest. The two knights reined in their mounts, and Dupres turned to her. "You are so like your father. Show her the proof."

The other knight slipped a small leather pouch off his belt and handed it to her. When she continued to stare at it, he urged, "Open it."

She recognized the pouch. It had belonged to Grandfather de Chauret. It held a family heirloom that had been gifted to her mother on the day she married Aimory de Chauret. With trembling hands, she did as the knight bade her. The gold cross slipped into her hands.

Her eyes lifted to meet the two men who had spent the last seven years protecting her mother while her father was serving England's new King William. She turned the cross over and read the engraving on the back—her grandfather's creed: *Aut Vincam, Aut Periam—I will either conquer or perish!*

"I must go to her, but what of my cousin? Will you send word to Augustin explaining why my plans have changed?"

Dupres whistled, and a group of men emerged from the forest. "Aye, we'll send a message."

The tone of his voice warned her something was wrong, but she was distracted by the men surrounding them. His fist shot out, and her head snapped back. The forest around her started to fade, but she fought to hang on to consciousness. She closed her eyes and let herself go limp in her captor's arms.

Her grandfather's cross grew warm in her hand, and she drew strength from his memory and his creed. She was a de Chauret, and she would fight. In her heart, she knew there would be one chance to act. Genvieve silently vowed to escape—or die trying!

MacInness scratched behind his horse's ear. "Nearly home, Duncan."

His horse lifted his head in response, and MacInness chuckled. "What more could a mon want or need than a flagon of mead, a lusty wench—or two—and his trusted destrier?" As he rode, the sounds of the forest stilled. In the eerie silence that followed, a scream rent the air, echoing through the night.

His protective instincts homed in on the sound. He whirled his horse around as a second scream was quickly silenced. Leaning low over his mount, the Highlander urged his horse faster. They burst through the trees in time to see a midnight-haired lass surrounded by a group of men.

Drawing closer, he could see her bruises. *Bloody buggers!* He pulled his claymore from the sheath on his back and swung the blade. Two attackers fell dead. As he aimed for the third, he saw the archer nock an arrow to his bow. He pressed his massive thighs to Duncan's sides to change direction, but the archer anticipated the movement and loosed his arrow.

At the last moment, MacInness leapt free as his horse went down. The bloody bastards would pay for killing his horse, but first he had to rescue an angel.

CHAPTER ONE

"Hang on, lass," MacInness urged. "'Tis just through the wood."

Shards of pain splintered throughout his bruised and battered body. His grip slackened. Ruthlessly pushing the pain aside, he focused on the woman in his arms and tightened his hold.

Ebony tresses lay plastered against her ghastly pale face. His throat closed. Was he too late? "Almost there," he rasped.

Refusing to give in to his body's clamoring need to stop and rest, Scots Mercenary, Winslow MacInness, clenched his jaw and his resolve. If he stopped now, he'd drop from sheer exhaustion. He'd not give the bastards the satisfaction of dying. Not now when sanctuary lay just across the open field.

Merewood Keep.

He crossed toward the Saxon holding. He'd been gone for months. Though he wished he'd stayed on in the Highlands, fate had brought him home and had him rescuing the woman he carried.

Would she make it? *Duncan hadn't.* He must be losing his mind as well as his life's blood if he was thinking about his dead horse.

Numbness crept slowly up his shins and his mind drifted. Not paying attention, he slipped on the wet grass, going down hard on one knee. The jagged edge of a rock tore into his flesh. Pain shot through him. Thank God he still had feeling in his legs.

"Hold!" a voice commanded through the mist.

Ignoring it, he placed one quivering leg in front of the other. If he stopped now, he'd never make it. He glanced down; she was still unconscious.

Too long.

The gash on his forehead began to throb in earnest, accompanied by the warm trickle of blood sliding down the side of his face.

The first arrow surprised him. He braced for another. The tip of the second arrow sliced through the bottom edge of his plaid before plunging into the soft earth between his feet. The feathered knock brushed against the top of his thigh and his manly pride.

"*Bollocks,*" he swore.

The lads are gettin' better. He shifted his handhold freeing his right hand and gave the signal Garrick taught him when he had sworn allegiance and become vassal to the Lord of Merewood Keep. Raising his fist in the air, he waited a heartbeat, then touched it to his heart.

The third arrow sailed wildly over his head and a voice called out, "MacInness?"

"Aye."

"We thought you dead." Garrick's shout was echoed by the grating of wood against stone as the gate opened.

"No' yet." His vision grayed as the blood oozing from a dozen places reached a crucial level. Darkness danced at the edge of his sight.

His legs wobbled, forcing him to his knees. The impact jarred the deep wound in his thigh. Razor sharp pain lanced through him as the healing wound re-opened. He gasped for breath.

"Let me help." A disembodied voice said while questing hands reached for the battered woman still held protectively in his arms.

"Nay." He fought off a surge of dizziness, pulling her closer to his heart.

"You cannot even hold yourself up. Let me take the woman."

He focused his gaze and looked into his overlord's eyes. "I canna," he whispered half to himself. "She'll die."

He closed his eyes against the harsh reality. After finally saying aloud what he'd feared while making his way back to Merewood, anguish lanced through him. Somehow, he knew if he severed the physical connection of her limp body tucked against his, she'd let go of the last thread of life she clung to.

MacInness had never seen anyone so fragile looking suffer so much and yet live to tell of it.

"Winslow?" A soft lilting voice called to him through the fog of pain threatening to swallow him whole.

"Jillie lass," he murmured.

"Aye," Garrick's wife answered. "You trust me, do you not?"

"What about—" Garrick started to protest.

MacInness opened one eye and saw the glare Merewood's lady bestowed upon her husband, and the answering look of retribution reflected back at her. He almost smiled.

"With my life, lass," he answered.

"And your friend's as well?" she asked, all the while prying his stiff fingers apart, one at a time.

His gut clenched. "I wilna let her suffer." He was too exhausted to care that his voice broke over the words.

"Let me ease her pain," she urged. "I've brought my healing herbs."

Garrick knelt down, waiting. MacInness slowly nodded to his overlord and then looked at Jillian. "Take away her pain, lass. I couldna."

Jillian nodded and touched the tips of her slender fingers to his brow. MacInness sighed and gratefully gave up his hold on the ebony-haired woman in his arms and let the pain have him.

⋙✺⋘

THE VOICE STOPPED. Her mind struggled to work its way through the cobwebs filling it.

The soothing cadence that had helped her hang on since the brutal attack slowly faded until the last words she recalled were, "I'm sorry."

Her body felt heavy, weighted down. She struggled against the need to sleep and fought to regain consciousness. Aches and pains assaulted her from different parts of her body. She felt as if she had been through a battle of epic proportions, battered about with a cudgel.

She slowly pried one eye open, and the room gradually came into focus. The wooden walls were planked…they looked new. She shifted and realized her head rested on something soft. She reached a hand around to touch the pillow; the movement releasing the faint but familiar scent of lavender. Turning her head to the side, she noticed a bowl and cloth lay on the table next to the bed, within reach. But the stool beside the bed was empty. A warm draft of air blew across her face. Instinctively, she turned toward the flames crackling in the brazier.

Sensing she was not alone, she turned her head. A woman stood staring out of the arrowslit, her delicate hand holding back the coarse cloth covering it. She did not know her. Her coloring marked her as Saxon or Scot with hair the color of fire and skin much too pale to be Norman.

Hearing the movement, the woman turned around. "Good," she said. "You are awake."

The words poised upon a shaft of pain before they lanced right through her head. She closed her eyes, fighting back tears of agony.

Three more knights emerged through the woods, bows drawn and battle ready. Strong arms lifted her off her feet and held tight, while her rescuer bounded over a log in their path. She wanted to look back to see if his horse was still alive, though she knew the enemy arrow had pierced its brain.

"This will help the ache in your head."

She opened her eyes and the woman leaned over her.

She shook her head and her belly clenched in agony. Her brave rescuer was gone.

Had they killed him? Was she being held captive? Were they going to drug her to keep her quiet?

Her mother's familiar warning arrowed through her aching head: *Trust not the Saxons.* She shook her head to clear it.

The red-haired woman took a step back and tilted her head to one side. The look on her face was confused at first, but then she started to smile. "I would never hurt a friend of Winslow's. I trust him with my life, as you have trusted him with yours," the woman paused, moving toward her once again.

"Won't you tell me your name and where you are from?" The woman's gentle tone soothed the frazzled nerves that quivered nonstop.

She opened her mouth to speak, but nothing came out. She tried again, but this time a brutally sharp pain speared through her throat. She grabbed it with both hands and could feel the swelling. Fear enveloped her. *Mon Dieu*, she could not speak!

"You've hurt your throat," the woman said. "Don't worry, you'll heal, if you'll just drink some of the herbal draught I mixed for you."

The realization that she could not speak swept through her like a blast of wind coming down from the north, chilling her to the bone. She started shaking.

The woman pulled the linen cover up to her chin and tucked it around her. "My name is Jillian," she said softly, coaxingly. "This is my home, Merewood Keep, and you are a guest here."

Her body was weak and in pain. The shock of her situation had waves of panic welling up from the pit of her belly. She was injured, far from home, but where was Merewood Keep? Her breaths became shorter and more rapid until her head started to spin.

The woman, Jillian, she remembered, took her quaking hands in her own and held them, quietly murmuring words in a foreign tongue. She had no idea what language it was, but some of the words sounded oddly familiar.

"I was taught to heal when I was very young," Jillian explained quietly. "People would come from great distances just to have my mother lay her healing hands upon them."

"I do not boast when I tell you that I, too, have that same ability," she continued softly. "I will do all in my power to help you heal. Please, drink this," Jillian handed the cup to the injured woman. "If you but rest, your body would have a better chance to heal."

Afraid, but overwhelmed by pain, she took the cup and sipped. The taste was one she recognized as a healing herb. The soothing effects were immediate. She patted her throat, blinking back tears of frustration.

"I'll send Winslow up, mayhap seeing him again will ease your mind."

The door closed with a muffled click. Silence echoed through the chamber.

"My name is Genvieve," she said again, still no sound emerged. One tear slipped past her guard, and then another. Her head and throat throbbed, and her body ached in more places than she remembered possessing.

Only one thought kept her from going out of her mind. She had to find the man who'd rescued her. Genvieve wondered if he would know this Winslow her hostess kept referring to.

Weariness engulfed her. Her eyes were growing very heavy thanks to the herbal draught she was given. She stopped fighting against the inevitable and let them close.

Her last conscious thought surprised her. Amber, her rescuer's eyes were the same pale golden brown as her father's best cognac. Smiling, she drifted off to sleep. But her sleep was not a relief. Genvieve tossed and turned while the nightmare held her in its cruel talons.

"You'll come with us now!" Beefy hands wrapped around her

wrists.

She was pulled off her horse...trapped...but not helpless. "Nay!" she shouted back. "My father—"

"Is in Abernathy with King William," her captor taunted.

"My mother—"

"Will stop at nothing to keep you from joining your cousin and his Saxon slut!" Dupres's sneer of triumph sliced her aching heart.

"Nay!" she shouted, denying it.

"SILENCE HER!" Another of her captors bellowed.

She turned to shout at him, but white-hot pain slashed across her throat. The man's elbow hit it dead center. Before she could draw in a breath, pain exploded at the back of her head and blackness engulfed her.

She tried to claw her way free from her dreams but could not seem to open her eyes. Was it a nightmare, or did it truly happen? *Mon Dieu*, she was not sure. Fear of being alone, trapped in horrific dreams, and unable to speak, speared through her. She whimpered.

"Have a care, lass." The cherished sound of the familiar, deep baritone crooned. "I'll no' let them hurt ye."

The voice was back, promising not to let anyone hurt her, and she believed him.

Genvieve smiled, snuggled deeper into the warmth of his familiar embrace, and drifted off to sleep.

※

MacInness settled the now sleeping woman more comfortably in his arms. The stitches running the length of his biceps pulled, but he ignored them. His broken ribs burned like the very devil, but he pushed the pain aside. The lass needed him.

A warm sensation, in the vicinity of his heart, spread through his chest as a feeling of well-being slowly enveloped him. It was somehow right holding her in his arms. She fit. He was starting to feel protective and territorial where the lass was concerned. But as soon she healed, he would walk away and return to his position as vassal to Garrick of Merewood.

An empty, hollow feeling started to spread through him at the very thought of leaving the fragile woman cradled in his battered arms. 'Tis the same that I feel for my sisters, he tried to reason, but his heart whispered that it was so much more.

"She still needs me," he said aloud. "'Tis all."

The empty room mocked him. His heart pounded out its denial with each successive beat. He knew it was not just the need to bed a warm and willing body; what he felt for the woman in his arms was not mere lust. The breath snagged in his chest as he realized he'd felt these feelings for a woman once before. The Lady Jillian—the woman he vowed to protect with his life. Uncomfortable with the emotions churning in his gut, he leaned toward the bed intending to lay her down.

"Winslow?" The object of his thoughts called from the doorway, a tray perched upon her hip.

He turned and straightened at the sound of his name on her lips. His overlord's wife stood there watching him with a small smile playing about her generous mouth. He groaned inwardly. She was his liege's wife…nay, he amended, his friend's wife. He had struggled long and hard to tamp down and conquer the feelings he had for her. It had been agony. She was a courageous woman, fair of face with a healing touch. She had captured his heart when she had been put under his protection while they had journeyed to where she wed his lord and friend, Garrick of Merewood.

His mouth thinned to a grim line as he recalled how he had hoped to change her mind and convince her to marry him instead. But it was not to be. In the end he had come to his senses and realized she did not love him. Though theirs was an arranged marriage, she truly loved the man she was to wed.

"Has someone slipped you a bit of unripe fruit?" Jillian smiled at him, her warm brown eyes mirroring the true depth of her unspoken concern.

He watched her walk toward him, careful not to upset the tray she carried.

"*Och* nay, lass." MacInness grinned. He could not help it; Lady Jillian's purity of spirit still had the power to move him. The woman in his arms moaned out again in her sleep. He shifted her gently until her cheek lay flush against his bandaged chest.

Uneasy with the longing that suffused him, he moved to set her aside, but she did something that made a lie out of every protest he grumbled out. The raven-haired beauty rubbed her face against him, sighed, and settled into a deeper sleep.

The feelings she stirred within him were sharp, akin to taking an arrow to the heart. He rubbed beneath his left collarbone. He still bore the scar where an arrow had thrust into his chest. MacInness definitely knew how the pain would feel. His breath whooshed in past his tightly clenched teeth. The woman in his arms sighed again. Holding her close to his heart felt like pure pleasure.

He groaned aloud.

Jillian dropped the tray. It bounced off the rushes and clattered against the wood floor. She was at his side in a heartbeat, poking and prodding him, searching for God knows what.

"I dinna think ye mean ta kill me, lass."

The change that came over the lady of the keep was instantaneous. All warmth receded, hiding behind the hurt in her eyes. "I thought you had opened the stitches in your arm," she huffed. "And promised I would bring something for the poor woman to eat."

Unnerved by her reaction, he teased, "Are ye thinkin' to scrape it out of the rushes?"

She flushed to the roots of her hair and bent to pick up the spilled contents from the tray. Bits of broken crockery mingled among the rushes with steaming chunks of venison, potato, and onion. As he watched, Jillian scooped up the ruined stew, blowing on her hands the whole while.

"Shouldna ye wait 'til it cools, lassie?" He watched for her reaction. It was not long in coming.

Slim hands clenched into tiny fists, hitting her hips with a vengeance. From her hostile, feminine pose, she had the grit to glare at him.

God help him, he could not hold it in. He laughed aloud. The pain was like a fire searing his battered body. He had to stop to catch his breath.

A soft sound recaptured his attention.

"Hush, lass," he soothed, stroking his fingertip across one eyebrow, then the other. Lush midnight lashes brushed against parchment-white skin, as her eyelids fluttered but stayed closed. He traced a line down the bridge of her nose with the tip of his battle-roughened forefinger.

"Hush now, *Mo Cridhe.*" My heart, the endearment rolled off his tongue. The woman sighed and burrowed against him, placing a small hand against his heart.

"MacInness!" Garrick called from the open doorway. "Has Jillian told you yet?"

He turned slowly toward the still-angry woman. "Told me what?"

"Nay," she whispered. "I have not."

"Things have changed at Merewood," Garrick told him.

MacInness stared at him and waited. Judging by the set of his overlord's face, the news was not good.

"Out with it, mon."

"Merewood has a new lord."

"And a fine job ye've been doin' of it."

Garrick shook his head. "You do not understand."

"Then ye'd best explain," MacInness demanded.

"While you were in Scotland, the king decided to gift Merewood to one of his barons… Augustin de Chauret."

MacInness felt his gut clench as his stomach began to roil, but he hid his reaction, nodding for his friend to continue.

"He has married my mother." Garrick hesitated. "Things are well here."

"But a Norman has control of your home." MacInness couldn't believe the man could calmly relate the news that he was no longer lord of the keep without emotion. "How can they be well?" MacInness demanded.

"Change comes," Jillian said, moving to stand beside her husband. "One must accept it and move on." When she reached out a hand to Garrick, he pulled her to his side.

MacInness nodded. "At least things are well with ye."

Garrick smiled slowly. "More than well, have you seen the babe?"

"Nay," MacInness answered. "I've been busy." He looked down at the woman in his arms. "Have you no word yet of anyone missin' a bride or a sister?" he asked, slowly standing intending to set the woman gently on the bed.

"Why do you ask?" Jillian prodded him, causing him to pause.

"She's young, and beneath the bruised and battered skin, verra beautiful." MacInness frowned. "Mayhap she was runnin' away…" he paused and looked meaningfully at Jillian, "from an unwanted husband."

Jillian ignored the intended barb. "I was not running away from Garrick, I was …" Her voice drifted off, and she looked at her husband.

"Not cooperative," he finished, reminding them of her flight to London to meet with the king to try to save her home and gift it to Garrick in return for her freedom.

"I am needed in the kitchens," she said in a strangled voice. "Call me if she wakens."

When she left the room, Garrick pulled the stool over next to the bed and motioned MacInness toward the bed. Once MacInness laid the woman down on it, Garrick said, "Jillian tells me the woman cannot speak. We still don't know who she is."

"'Tis a wonder the blow to her throat didna break her neck." MacInness shook his head. It was a miracle she survived.

Disbelief flickered in Garrick's penetrating gaze "You saw it happen?"

He nodded. "But I was too far away. By the time I reached her, she had taken a blow to the back of the head, as well." He hurt just remembering the brutal force of the blows and her one sharp cry of pain before she crumbled into a heap on the ground.

"We'll find out who she is," Garrick reassured him. "It won't be long before she can tell us."

"Aye," MacInness agreed, though he had an uncomfortable feeling that the situation was already far beyond their control. Whoever she belonged to could be out searching for her even now. "What of your new duties?" he asked, changing the subject, not wanting to dwell on having to let the dark-haired woman go.

"Augustin de Chauret is a fair man."

MacInness wondered why the new lord of the keep hadn't been by to question him and asked, "Where is he?"

"In London."

"And while he's gone?" MacInness prompted, wondering if his thickheaded friend would tell him what he really wanted to know.

"He is content to share the duties involved in the running of the Keep."

"But what of your men?" MacInness asked. "How do they feel about the Norman warriors in their midst?"

Garrick laughed and shook his head, "That would be a tale worth repeating over more than one cup of Merewood's fine mead."

MacInness sensed there was more that Garrick wasn't telling him.

"I'd like you to see for yourself how well the two groups work together," he said. "Now that they have stopped trying to slip a dirk between one another's ribs." He rubbed the back of his neck.

MacInness glanced over to the bed, satisfying himself that she slept peacefully. "I'm sorry to have missed it. Do ye still have a place for me and my men?"

"Need you ask?" Garrick placed a hand on the Scot's shoulder.

MacInness smiled and shook his head. "I've yet to deliver the missive from Roderick," he said slowly, looking for the sealed bit of parchment he'd tucked next to his heart.

"Since he is not here," Garrick said, "I can only guess he was detained by a pretty face."

"*Och*, ye could say that." MacInness drew out the telling, cursing his inability to just blurt it out. He did not know how Garrick would take the news that they were now related by marriage.

As if he sensed trouble, Garrick asked, "What happened?"

MacInness cleared his throat. "Yer youngest brother is a married mon."

Garrick's shock was palpable. "Roderick?"

"Aye," MacInness groaned, "to a little bit of a thing with hair red as fire and temper to match yer darlin' wife."

Garrick's eyes narrowed, "Handfasted?" he asked.

MacInness knew then that Garrick had reasoned out part of it. There was no point in keeping the rest from him, but he really was not up to arguing today. "Can ye no' just read it, then?"

"Do you know what it says?" Garrick asked, his expression closed.

"*Och* no, ye know I canna read."

"Are we to be brothers, then?" Garrick asked haltingly.

MacInness admired his friend's ability to reason out the situation. "I ne'er could keep anythin' from ye."

"'Tis me cousin, Alwyne. She's lived with my family since she was a bairn. Her father, my father's younger brother, died when she was just three summers, her mother when she was born."

Garrick nodded, waiting for him to continue.

"If it wasna for Black Doughal's accusations, questioning Alwyne's honor, there wouldna been a need for her to marry." MacInness could not help but smile, remembering the way young Roderick had stood up to Clan Gordon's fiercest warrior. "Ye'd be proud of Roderick, he fought well."

Garrick shook his head. "Mayhap we should skip the training and head right to the mead," he groaned. "This sounds like a long-winded tale."

MacInness turned back to the woman and the bed. Unable to stop himself, he brushed a lock of midnight hair off her forehead, stroking a fingertip along the curve of her cheek.

"Sleep, lass," he whispered, then turned and headed for the door.

The soft sound of her even breathing soothed the worry roiling in his gut. Who was she? Where did she come from?

And God help them, would Merewood's defenses be ready when her people came looking for her?

Chapter Two

"Where are they?" Annaliese de Chauret demanded.

The man on his knees before her continued to cower but did not change his reply. "I do not know, milady."

"Send Jacques to me," she snapped.

The woman standing off to her right nodded and left to do her bidding. Moments later, a tall knight, with blue-black hair and a wicked-looking scar slashing across the entire side of his face, approached the agitated woman.

"Milady?" he said simply, waiting for her to speak.

"Bien," she said. "Now that you are here, I am assured that my bidding shall be done."

"What do you wish?" he asked.

"Find my daughter and bring her home," Lady Annaliese murmured in a quiet voice. "Stop at nothing to ensure that she never reaches Merewood Keep. My brother's son will have to find someone else to watch his child."

Jacques bowed low before her and turned to leave.

"One moment," she called out. "I do not wish her to be harmed. The last man I sent to do the job has not yet returned."

"Dupres?" he asked.

"Oui, I sent the wrong man after my daughter the first time," she paused, pinning him with a glare. "I am certain that I have not made another error in judgment. Do not return without my

Genvieve."

With a nod, she dismissed him.

With a bow, he was gone.

⇶⇷

"Milord," Armand called out.

Augustin de Chauret turned and waited for the warrior to catch up to him. When the young knight slowed his destrier to a halt beside him, Augustin nodded for him to speak.

"Your cousin, Genvieve, has not been seen for almost a fortnight."

Augustin's jaw clenched in reaction to the news. It was as he had feared. "Go on," he urged.

"I did as you bid, but neither search party has found her." Armand paused in his report to remove the small leather pouch that hung from his belt. He dumped the contents into the palm of his hand.

Augustin's breath caught in his throat. The gold cross lay dull and lifeless in Armand's hand. It was identical to the one his uncle had given to his wife—Genvieve's mother—the day they wed. Almost afraid of the truth, he hesitantly reached out and turned the piece over. As he had feared, his grandfather's creed was engraved on the back, *Aut Vincam, Aut Periam. I will either conquer or perish.*

He reached out and took the cross from the warrior. "Where did you find this?"

Something akin to sorrow swiftly flashed across the younger man's features. Augustin knew the rest of the report would not be welcome.

"Near the remnants of a campfire, two days north of Merewood." He cleared his throat. "There were signs of battle," he finished in a low voice.

Augustin fingered the cross, and wondered how his aunt's most prized piece of jewelry would come to be so close to his new holding? And why would there be signs of battle? Augustin was unsure he would ever know.

"*Bien*," he said finally acknowledging the end of Armand's report. "I have satisfied my liege's curiosity for the time being. The king is pleased with the continued prosperity at Merewood Keep."

"Lady Eyreka should be pleased," Armand said.

Augustin nodded. "Have the men ready to begin the journey home at dawn," Augustin said. He watched the warrior spur his destrier and head back toward the castle while his mind churned with unanswered questions.

He turned his own mount to follow.

CHAPTER THREE

GENVIEVE WOKE WITH a start. Her eyes flew open, and for an instant, she could not remember where she was. Then it hit her; she did not know where she was. Nay, she thought, she had heard Lady Jillian say she was at Merewood Keep. Merewood…why was the name so familiar?

The dull ache at the back of her skull picked up tempo and throbbed in earnest when she tried to remember where she had heard the name. The blow to her head must be muddling her thoughts, but one thought slashed through the fog, *I won't give up, even if it hurts to think!*

The silence in the room was deafening, and the realization she could do nothing to break through that silence made her heart pound and her chest grow taut with fear. Dozens of questions swirled around in her aching head. But only two had the power to drive her to the depths of despair and the brink of madness: *How in the name of God would she be able to survive if she could not speak?* Her hands clenched the bed linens until her knuckles ached. Glancing down, she saw they were white with strain. A line of sweat beaded on her upper lip. She swiped at it with the sleeve of her borrowed sleeping gown. *How would she get word to her parents that she was safe?*

The room started to fade out of focus, and a disturbing buzz began to sound in her ears.

Genvieve gritted her teeth and clenched her jaw, hanging on to consciousness. *"Aut vincam,"* her mind screamed, while she tried to say the words aloud to no avail. The effort to be heard cost her; she was limp from the exertion. She gingerly touched her throat and winced. It was still so tender to the touch. It had to be badly bruised on the inside as well. But what would happen when it healed? Would she regain the use of her voice?

Mon Dieu, she did not know.

※

MacInness was not certain he believed the man in front of him was capable of accepting Garrick's men-at-arms and household knights, let alone the Saxon people of Merewood Keep. When his friend suggested MacInness observe the training session, he hadn't intended to participate since his injuries were still fresh.

But as MacInness eyed the gray-haired warrior, one of de Chauret's vassals, with equal disdain, he silently measured the man for a box made of pine. Hell, he'd even help dig the hole to bury him, he thought then smiled. A pity the Norman would have to die, he almost admired the way the man had with a battle-axe.

"Then you'd like to test your strength against mine?" the Norman asked.

"My pleasure." MacInness unconsciously assumed his battle-stance, his body taut as a coil, ready to spring to the attack.

The other warrior, Henri, didn't back away. In fact, he took a step closer, so that they were nose to nose. MacInness was almost impressed. At his snort of laughter, all sound ceased and movement in the lower bailey came to an abrupt halt.

Warriors and stable hands stood side by side, quietly waiting for the impending fight. Henri drew his sword first, but MacInness was quick to answer the challenge. He drew out his claymore and swung it above his head before gripping it with both hands to land a savage blow to the warrior's side.

Henri reeled back from the impact and his expression had MacInness smiling. He knew the Norman was impressed. The mon should be. In a lightning-fast move, MacInness had the warrior off-balance. Taking full advantage, he sheathed his claymore, and started to push the warrior over with his free hand.

It was MacInness's turn to be surprised. The Norman grabbed MacInness's hand and righted himself. But before Henri could land a blow with his broadsword, MacInness had his dirk poised in the hollow of the man's throat.

"I'd hate to kill ye," MacInness growled. "Ye're almost a worthy opponent."

"Enough," Garrick bellowed. MacInness closed his eyes and swore, but he obeyed, slipping the dirk back into its leather sheath.

"When I asked you to join the morning's training session, I did not think you'd try to kill one of our vassals," Garrick bit out.

MacInness took a step back, brushing his unruly red hair out of his eyes. "I hadna planned to." He'd rot in hell before he admitted why he would have killed the man.

He'd overheard Henri insulting the woman he rescued. Since Lady Jillian had barred everyone from the solar, MacInness knew that the Norman had not seen the injured woman, so there was no reason for the Norman to hold such a low opinion of the poor lass.

MacInness felt protective of her and her honor. It did not matter what had happened to her before he came upon the infidels beating her. She didn't deserve the beating, and she didn't deserve Henri's disdain. So, he accepted the offer to train with the men, and if the Norman was foolish enough to accept the challenge, then it wasn't MacInness's fault if the mon died because of his lack of ability.

Garrick took the other warrior aside and spoke to him. Whatever was said would obviously stay between them. Henri nodded and stalked away.

"Patrick," Garrick called out, "MacInness volunteered to ride out on patrol this morning."

MacInness glared at his friend but did not contradict him. He'd save that for later. He was tired, his head a bit muddled from the mead they'd had to drink before coming to the bailey, but he'd cut out his tongue before he admitted to a weakness.

As the group disbanded, MacInness had to admire how quickly Garrick had diffused the situation. Although he would rather have taken a piece out of the Norman's hide first.

"You won't want to get on the wrong side of that one," Patrick said nodding toward the retreating warrior. "He's de Chauret's right hand man, not too slow with sword or fist," Patrick added with a twinkle in his eye, as they entered the cool, dim stable.

"I dinna want to be on his right side, either," MacInness said sullenly, saddling the horse Garrick insisted he use. He was racking his brain trying to reason out why he had reacted so strongly to the Norman's words.

"Does everyone think she's a leman?" he asked the tall Irishman. The Norman's slighting comments about the dubious reputation of the woman he rescued bothered him to the point where he'd been ready to kill to protect the woman's honor.

"'Twas dark when you brought her in, and Lady Jillian had her settled in the solar before anyone else knew she was there."

"She was badly injured," MacInness said slowly, the memory of those injuries plagued him still.

"You'd think from the way Lady Jillian keeps everyone away that the woman has something to hide."

MacInness shrugged. He didn't know any more than Patrick, hadn't had the time to find out while they were on the run from whomever had attacked the lass.

Patrick frowned at him. "Does it matter?"

MacInness wondered why it should. He didn't know anything about her other than she had long dark hair and beneath her bruises was very beautiful. As they led their horses through

Merewood's gates, MacInness admitted, "I canna answer ye yet. I feel—" he said and stopped.

What did he feel? Why did the woman addle his brain to the point where he was defending her honor before he even knew who or what she was?

Patrick looked over his shoulder at the group of men riding out to join them. "In the ten summers I have ridden with you, I've only seen you this way once before."

"Dinna even start," MacInness ground out, sensing what his second in command was about to say.

Patrick nodded. "When you are ready to talk, I'm ready to listen." With that he urged his horse into a canter with his heels.

MacInness waited a few moments, allowing the others to follow behind Patrick, before he too picked up the pace.

⇶⇷

GENVIEVE WANTED TO heave the tray across the room at the dense serving girl. Short of doing that there was no way to get the girl to pay attention to her. It seemed that since the young woman knew Genvieve could not speak, she ignored her and carried on her own one-sided conversation.

Genvieve was tired of hearing what she should and should not do in order to regain her strength. Finally, the servant left, after tucking the covers around Genvieve for the third time. The room had grown steadily darker with the approaching night. A pale shaft of light spilled through the arrowslit, illuminating a few floorboards next to the bed where she lay.

If I stay here one more moment, I shall go mad! Genvieve was sick to death at hearing the words inside of her head instead of aloud.

The sound of raised voices drifted in on the night air. She drew in a deep breath and was rewarded with the heady scent of rain in the air. The breeze changed and had a sudden chill to it.

We need rain, she thought, no longer trying to use her voice to speak. It hurt her throat too much. *Mayhap if I give my voice a rest, it will come back more quickly.*

Swinging her legs out over the edge of the bed, she slipped off and stood. Though her legs were shaky from fatigue, they held her up once she locked her knees. Grabbing the woolen wrap off the top of the chest near the wall, she pulled it around her shoulders. Though still summer, the nights had grown noticeably cooler as of late.

A wave of dizziness threatened to send her to her knees, but she put a hand to the wall and waited until it passed. Steadier, she opened the door a crack and checked to see if anyone stood outside. A fair-haired young warrior stood near the top of the stairs. He looked vaguely familiar, but Genvieve could not place where she had seen him. Her memory had definitely suffered from the blow to the head. Trying to remember anything beyond the present moment was an effort.

As she watched, someone called out from the darkened hall below, and the warrior quickly descended. Genvieve knew she had only a few moments, if at all, before the man returned to stand guard. Slipping out of the chamber, she followed the steps to the floor below. Standing in the darkened hall, fear overwhelmed her and for a few heart-stopping moments she could not see a way out. Her gaze swept the room and finally noticed a faint light near the floor on the other side of the hall.

Her bare feet made no sound as she ran across the vast room. Once on the other side, she paused to catch her breath, placing her ear against the door to listen. Nothing. Pulling the door open, she slipped outside and down the stone steps.

Freedom.

She darted across the bailey toward the shadows of the stable yard. Lord, she had no idea it would feel quite so liberating to be outside the hall. A gust of wind whipped past her, accompanied by a flash of light.

Genvieve froze in her tracks. The answering rumble of thunder had her quaking with fear. *Just a summer storm*, she reasoned with herself, trying to overcome the fear that gripped her every time she heard the deep rumble or sharp crack of thunder. It has always been thus, since the storm that had uprooted two ancient trees and shaken the foundations at her family's holding in Rouen. The first fat drops of rain were all the warning she got before the skies opened up. She was soaked before she could seek cover.

No longer anxious to escape, she headed for the stable to get out of the driving rain. She shivered and looked about her. A few horses were curious enough to poke their heads over their stall doors, but after sniffing the air they lost interest and ignored her. Genvieve sank to her knees in the corner on a sweet-smelling pile of hay. She grew colder by the moment; sorry that she ventured out at night, but even more sorry that she hadn't been able to get away.

Her eyes drifted closed, though the shivers racking her body did not cease. Exhaustion finally claimed her, and she feel into a deep, dreamless sleep.

Chapter Four

MACINNESS STOOD AND stared at the still-soaked, bedraggled woman asleep in the hay.

Did the lass lose all of her sense when she was hit on the head? What was she doing out of bed? What was she doing out of her chamber in the middle of the night during a storm?

He tried to rouse her. "Lass, can ye hear me?"

The woman moaned and Winslow cursed. "Dinna tell me, ye've taken ill, too," he ground out. "I already *ken* ye've lost yer mind."

A soft whinny sounded from the stall to the left of him. He replied, "Aye, she is a stubborn one at that," he said to the horse.

Lifting her into his arms, he shook his head, and fighting the urge to bellow the words, rasped, "Ye'll catch yer bloody death, lying about, soaked to the bone."

A flash of lightning illuminated her face. Black eyelashes fluttered, and she opened her eyes. Her brow furrowed in confusion. She squirmed in his arms, and he wanted to reassure her, "Yer safe now, lass." He stroked a hand across her forehead.

He drew back his hand in shock expecting her to be cool to the touch, but her body was hot as blazes. She had a fever.

"Why, in God's name, are ye lying out here, when ye've a perfectly good bed in Lady Jillian's solar?" Anger sharpened his tone. She winced and tried to turn her head away from him.

MacInness touched the tip of his finger beneath her chin and turned her face toward him. "*Och*, don't mind me, lass," he said in a gentler tone. "I was worried for ye. I have to find Lady Jillian; she'll know what to do for yer fever."

Making his way back across the bailey, he cursed whatever fates had placed her in his path. He did not want to have these feelings stirring around in his gut again. She irritated him and intrigued him. An all too familiar combination that had nearly led to his downfall a year ago.

He'd learned his lesson well. At nine and twenty, he had fallen in love for the first time ... though the one he loved was pledged to another. No amount of persuasion on his part had convinced Lady Jillian that he was the one she was destined to love.

Now here he was in danger of repeating the same mistake, only this time, he did not know who the woman was. For all he knew she could already be married! That black thought had him cursing beneath his breath and tightening his hold on the slender woman in his arms. The need to shelter and protect her overwhelmed him because whoever her husband was had failed to do so. Why else would the poor wee lass have been under attack?

He clenched his jaw to keep from blurting out questions he knew the woman could not answer. He'd not fail in his bid to protect her. And if she were married, he thought, he'd let her go, but not until he'd taken the mon aside and given him the benefit of his years as a warrior and instructed him in how to take care of his wife.

As he walked, she settled against him and a nagging thought prodded at him. Would he be able to protect his heart from her? Making his way across the bailey and up the steps to the hall, he realized what he had to do until he found out more about her.

Distance, he thought. Distance from the distraction was the answer.

TWO DAYS LATER, MacInness stood in the doorway of her chamber. "How is the lass?" he asked in low tones.

"The fever still has her," the young woman answered.

"I'm verra sorry, but I dinna recall yer name," MacInness said, walking into the room.

"Simone," the young woman answered.

"I havena seen ye here before," MacInness observed.

"I came with Angelique and usually work in the kitchens," she said, smiling up at him. Wringing the linen cloth, she placed it back upon the woman's brow. "Sara is helping Lady Jillian deliver a babe," she said. "Gert could spare me so here I am."

MacInness nodded, wondering who Angelique was but he had other worries right now. His gut knotted up, as he asked, "Did Lady Jillian say anything about her fever?"

"Nay," Simone answered. "But two days is not so long to have a fever," she paused in her ministrations and glanced up. "She is strong; her body is still fighting it."

MacInness could not speak past the lump in his throat. Clearing it, he thanked the young woman. He wondered briefly if this was how the lass felt, not being able to speak.

He shook his head. "Distance," he muttered to himself, slipping back out of the chamber.

Three days later, he was enjoying a cup of mead with Garrick and Patrick when their conversation was interrupted by a resounding crash from above. All three men paused, a heartbeat later another crash followed.

Rising to his feet, MacInness sprinted toward the stairs. The woman's fever had broken and she was on the mend. What could possibly be wrong now? He took the stairs two at a time with Garrick and Patrick coming up the stairs behind him.

He paused at the door to the solar long enough to catch an armful. The young woman's startled expression changed to one of indignation, "She just started throwing things at me," she said with a quiver in her voice.

"Who did?" MacInness asked steadying the young woman on her feet.

The serving girl started to answer, but instead darted behind MacInness, as another object was hurled from across the room.

MacInness growled low in his throat and stalked into the room. The sight awaiting him robbed him of his ability to breathe. The flushed young woman, standing atop the bed, commanded all of his attention. Her midnight hair hung about her shoulders in wild disarray, her gray-green eyes sparking with temper. God, she was beautiful. His breath whooshed out and his tongue got tied. Watching the emotions rioting across the woman's face he realized, while his reaction to Lady Jillian had been similar, no other woman had ever affected him quite this way before.

Garrick pushed past him and walked toward the bed. Patrick nudged him aside and muttered something under his breath about women and half-witted Scots.

"What are ye thinkin', lassie?" MacInness asked approaching her. "Surely ye didna mean to throw that bowl at the poor wee thing?"

The scowl that the woman leveled at him was hot enough to singe his hair. He walked over to her, and she plopped down on the bed. Her quick glance at the other men told him she must have finally realized they were not alone. She yanked the covers up and glared at him.

MacInness shook his head.

She looked him in the eye and mouthed a curse that curled his toes. He shook his head; he must have imagined that she was cursing him.

He crouched down next to her, so that they were eye level. "Are ye in pain, lass?" he asked, concerned.

She raised her eyes to the ceiling, crossed her arms in front of her chest, and huffed.

"I'll take that as a no, then," MacInness said. He started to turn around to speak to Garrick, when he saw her move her mouth again. This time he was certain of it, she called him a bloody bastard. He stood very slowly and walked over to where Garrick stood speaking to Patrick. "I think the lass needs a change of company," he said carefully. "I'll be down to join ye shortly." The two men nodded and left the room.

MacInness paced from one side of the chamber to the other, still reeling from the realization that the woman would feel compelled to rain a curse down on his head. He shuddered to think of where she had heard the first curse she uttered. Turning back to face her, he was surprised to see her watching him intently.

"We've no' had the chance to be properly introduced, lass," he began. "My name is Winslow MacInness."

She nodded her understanding.

"I am the one who brought you here," he added.

Here? her lips formed the words, though no sound came forth.

"Aye," he said slowly, "Merewood Keep is in Northumbria, not so far from the Scottish border."

The woman shook her head, she seemed amazed.

"Why did ye throw those things at Sara?" he asked. "She was only trying to care for ye," he added.

The woman grabbed his hand in both of hers and pulled hard. She had his full attention. He tried not to be distracted by her beauty but it was nearly impossible. "Is there somethin' ye need then, lass?"

She nodded, and patted her throat, her eyes welling up with tears.

In spite of his decision to stay away from her, he was drawn in by the silent pleading in her gray-green gaze.

"Yer throat pains ye?" he asked, knowing that it should. Though it had been more than a few days since she was injured, he reasoned that the force of the blow should require more time to heal.

She nodded her agreement and opened her mouth to speak, then, as if realizing the futility, she closed her mouth and bowed her head.

MacInness had the overwhelming need to do something. He needed to help her find a way to communicate with others.

"Mayhap, I can help ye, lass," he said softly. "Are ye willing to try?" he asked, needing to know that she had the desire to work with him.

Her eyes were red-rimmed and her lashes heavy with unshed tears. The longing in her gaze cut right through his decision to maintain his distance from her. He was sucked in by her undeniable need. For the first time in MacInness's life, he was the sole focus of someone who desperately needed him. The feeling was not unwelcome; daunting, but not unwelcome.

He pulled the stool closer to the bed and patted her hands. "To start then, lass," he said. "How would you tell me yer hungry?" he asked.

She shook her head, but refused to open her mouth.

"Weel now, if ye canna speak, have ye another idea?"

She glared at him and mouthed another colorful word that MacInness swore no lady should know.

He shook his head. "I dinna think a lady would know such words, lass," he chastised her.

The woman dropped her gaze toward her lap, but not before he caught a wisp of a smile.

"Why can ye not put a hand to yer stomach?" he suggested.

She tilted her head to one side, as if considering and then patted her stomach.

"Fine," MacInness said encouraging her. "I'll know yer hungry."

"If yer thirsty," he asked, "what then?" he urged.

She put a hand to her throat, but MacInness shook his head. "I'll think yer throat pains ye."

She blew out a breath, crossed her arms in front of her, and frowned grumpily.

MacInness could not help smiling. "Ye could pretend to hold a cup and drink from it," he offered.

The woman smiled then. With her eyes sparkling and her face aglow, she was a sight to behold. MacInness felt his control slipping as he gazed at her. The cleft in her chin and tiny mole by her upper lip practically begged to be kissed.

He had to clear his throat to speak. "That's fine, then, lass," he said quietly. Taking the time to study her and knowing he'd be damned for his next words, he rasped, "Yer a welcome sight at the end of a long day, lass." Longing suffused his weary soul.

She placed a hand to her breast.

"Are ye surprised?" he asked.

She nodded.

"Well, ye shouldn't be," he admonished. "Ye've a rare beauty."

He paused, then mumbled to himself, "I wish I knew yer name."

She grabbed his arm and rapidly mouthed a few words.

MacInness shook his head, unable to understand what she was saying. Curse words, well now, they were more than familiar to him…but names, he'd have to work long and hard to figure out what she was saying.

"Can ye try again?" he urged.

He sat closer and concentrated on the movement of her lips, but instead of focusing on what she was saying, all he could do was think of kissing her rose-tinted lips. Imagining their fullness beneath his own set off a chain reaction that started with a hollow feeling in the pit of his stomach and had him shifting on the stool.

"I'm verra sorry, lass," he said in a gruff voice. "I canna understand ye. Is yer name not Saxon then?"

She shook her head.

"Is it Scots?"

She shook her head again … this time she started to huff with impatience.

"Are ye Norman?"

She hit the palm of her hand against her forehead.

MacInness laughed aloud. The woman had a sense of humor. "All right, then, tell me again…just one name this time."

Her mouth moved, and he was almost too distracted to follow what she was saying. It was no use; he could not make out what she was saying.

"I am verra sorry, lass," he took her hands in his. "I canna sort it out."

At her crestfallen look, he added. "There is a Norman maidservant working in the kitchen, mayhap she can help ye."

The woman's tremulous smile was all the reward he needed. She patted a hand to her stomach and then held an imaginary cup to her lips.

"Aye, lass," he said smiling. "I've a powerful hunger and thirst, too."

She pushed back the covers and started to swing her legs over the edge of the bed.

"*Och*…nay, lass," he said placing his hands on her knees. "Ye canna—" he started to say, but the rest of the words stuck in his throat.

The edge of her sleeping gown had caught beneath her and flashed a hint of creamy-smooth skin before she covered it. His hands tingled where they touched her petal smooth skin. His gaze shot up and waited for her to look at him. She stared at his hands, then raised her gaze to lock with his. Her skin was not as pale as the women in his family. Hers was a deeper shade that was turning a dusky rose along her high cheekbones, as he watched her breaths became shorter and more frequent. She was as affected as he.

The need to take her in his arms stopped him cold. He had been too long without a woman. She was a stranger. He didn't know who she was or where she came from. The only thing he did know was that he desired her with a passion that was growing out of control.

"I'll bring ye food and drink," he mumbled, pulling the covers up to her chin.

    She nodded, folded her hands in her lap and tried to smile. MacInness did not miss that fact that her hands shook, and wondered if he had been quick enough to hide that fact his did, too.

CHAPTER FIVE

GENVIEVE COULD NOT hold in the sigh that escaped the moment Winslow closed the chamber door. His very presence in the chamber made her skin tingle and the room go hot. Thoughts of him leaning down and capturing her lips in a bold kiss had desire pooling low in her belly. It had been years since she'd felt this way—since her husband died.

Uncomfortable with thoughts of her late husband, and shocked by the sensations reawakened by Winslow's hand gripping her knee, she needed to do something. *To move.*

Throwing the covers aside, she got out of bed, but her foot got tangled in her sleeping gown. Trying to brace herself with her hand at the last minute, she moaned as it folded beneath her.

Sharp pain sliced through her wrist. *Merde. I should have stayed in bed.* Standing slowly, she got back into bed and drew the covers up to her chin. Her wrist didn't look any different. It would be all right. Wanting to be ready when Winslow returned, she put her hand down and pushed herself up straighter on the bed. The bolt of agony shooting up her arm through her wrist brought tears to her eyes.

At least the pain in my hand can take my mind off the pain in my head and throat.

Cradling her hand to her side, she wondered what she'd say to anyone who asked how she hurt it. *As I cannot speak, there's* nothing to tell.

The silence was starting to eat away at her. She longed for Winslow's company. While she had not been able to speak to him, he had cared enough to try to understand what she tried to say. She did have elemental needs, but she also had the deep-rooted need to be with people, to speak to people. Two tears escaped, mirroring one another as they fell, sweeping down across her cheeks, before she brushed at them impatiently.

Winslow was the man who had rescued her; mayhap he could tell her what she could not remember. Where had he found her and who had abducted her? She dare not wonder the why of it yet. That could come later when she could speak again.

The door to the chamber swung open wide, and all rational thought fled. The breadth of Winslow's shoulders would not fit though the door, he had to turn slightly to enter the chamber.

His slow smile made her entire body start to quiver all over again. His flame-bright hair fell untamed to his shoulders and should have made him appear less a man. He looked so different than the close-cropped dark-haired Norman men. He appeared every inch the conquering Scots barbarian, and she was distinctly uncomfortable with the feelings he drew from deep within her.

The sensual lure in his golden-brown gaze pinned her to the bed. With a certainty, Genvieve knew he was attracted to her. She had seen the same look in Francois's dark eyes many, many times. She closed her eyes to block out the man before her, willing her mind to call up the vision of her dead husband. Though she tried, she could not quite bring his handsome features fully into focus. Francois's dark eyes, aquiline nose, and aristocratic features kept blurring. Her traitorous mind replaced them with a broad, freckled face, slightly crooked nose, and warm amber eyes.

Damn the man for making her feel desire again. She wasn't ready, and had no time to deal with such feelings. She was trapped by her body's need to fully recover from the attack. Until she had the strength to saddle a horse and to go home or could speak, she couldn't leave or ask which roads were safe to travel. Though she was loathe to admit it, she knew she could not travel alone and would be forced to stay at Merewood Keep a little longer.

The sound of a woman's low voice snapped Genvieve out of her reverie. Embarrassed for not noticing the slender serving woman who had accompanied Winslow, she looked down at her knees and smoothed the bed linens. The familiar motions soothed her, helping her to regain her composure.

"I've brought Simone to meet ye, lass," Winslow said, his voice low and soothing.

She nodded her head.

Winslow led the woman over to the bed. "Tell her yer name, lass," he commanded.

Genvieve, she mouthed.

Simone looked at her, and then up at Winslow, "I think she said Genvieve."

The vigorous nod of her head confirmed Simone's words.

"Genvieve," Winslow said, putting the accent on the first part of her name, rather than the last so it sounded more like *JAN veev*.

Genvieve smiled, it really didn't matter how he said her name. What mattered was that the people would have something else to call her, other than *that poor woman*.

"You are Norman," Simone said with a small smile.

Genvieve nodded.

"Do you live nearby?" Simone asked.

Genvieve shook her head. She wanted to tell the young woman that until recently, she had been living in London with her parents. She wanted to tell her that she had intended to join her cousin Augustin to help care for his young daughter, Angelique, but her handicap stopped her.

Winslow took hold of her hands and gently stroked them. Unconsciously, she pulled her injured hand back with a jerk.

"Let me ha' another look at yer hand, lass."

"Her name is Genvieve," Simone prodded him.

"Aye," Winslow agreed, "but her name gets caught around my Scots tongue…lass is easier." Though he directed his words to Simone, his gaze locked with Genvieve's, seeking her approval.

At her slow nod, he smiled warmly.

Held captive by his heated gaze, she didn't notice what Winslow was doing until he prodded the bones of her hand and wrist. A low moan escaped before she could stop herself.

"Simone, will ye fetch Lady Jillian?"

"*Oui*," she headed for the door.

"Tell her, I ha' need of her healin' herbs," Winslow told her.

Looking back at Genvieve, he added, "Lady Jillian has a concoction that will ease any swellin' or pain…a root of some kind."

Comfrey, she mouthed.

He watched her mouth move, but didn't respond. His amber eyes darkened a moment before he blinked and their color returned to normal.

"How did ye hurt yer hand?"

She shrugged in answer. She'd never tell him she'd been too unsettled by his touch to lay in bed, while thoughts of him getting into that bed with her drove her to the brink of madness.

He stared at her, as if willing her to speak. When she didn't, he sighed and told her, "Lady Jillian is a gifted healer, though Lady Eyreka is as well."

Genvieve frowned at him. They were not the only ones well versed in the art of healing, she had learned at her mother's knee. Her mother had taught her many things. Among them, how to run a vast holding, prepare a feast fit for a king, and care for a newborn babe.

A sharp, hollow pain pierced her breast at the thought of her miscarried babes. She had lost both early in her marriage to Francois and had not conceived again in the eight years that followed. Before she could bring herself back to the present, she heard Winslow call out to Lady Jillian.

With a brisk efficiency, the lady of the keep prepared the poultice. "How did you hurt your hand?" Lady Jillian asked quietly.

"Her name is Genvieve," Winslow urged.

The woman's eyes widened at the name, and she looked about to say something, but obviously changed her mind and merely nodded. Genvieve wondered if she should know Lady Jillian, or if the woman's reaction was to the odd way Winslow pronounced her name.

Winslow looked at her and then the other women and blurted out, "The lass took exception to somethin' I said."

Jillian smiled knowingly. "Well, I certainly cannot fault Genvieve. I have often felt that way myself," she finished with a chuckle. "I'll be back later to wrap your hand," she said before turning toward Winslow. "Do try not to say anything to encourage our guest to strike you again."

"Ye wound me sorely," he said, holding his hands to his heart.

Genvieve saw the other woman smile at the sincerity of his words, though Genvieve could not help but wonder if he truly meant what he said.

Winslow settled himself next to the bed and moved to hand Genvieve a trencher of food, then frowned when she tried to reach out with her injured hand.

"Ye need to hold that hand still, lass," he instructed.

She started to shake her head at him, but he ignored her and reached for her hand. "Ye canna let the poultice slide off," he gently stroked his thumb on the underside of her wrist.

Her gaze darted to his and understanding blossomed between them. He must have felt it too because his gaze darkened, as her pulse raced.

"Try using yer other hand."

Genvieve tried, but it was too awkward for her, reaching across her body to the tray resting on the table beside the bed. She sighed in frustration and dropped her hand back to her side.

Without a word, Winslow picked up a spoonful of stew, blew on it, and held it before her lips. She shook her head and pointed to the bowl of broth and bread.

"'Tis sorry I am, lass. I shouldha' realized yer throat pained yet to eat as well as speak." He dunked the bread in the bowl and mashed it with the spoon until it would be easier to swallow. She let him feed her, his large hands surprisingly gentle.

The tension eased out of her shoulders as he held the spoon and continued to feed her. In between bites, he ate, until at last their hunger had been satisfied.

Genvieve wanted to thank him, the need to speak aloud overwhelming her. But Winslow was looking away from her, and did not see her lips moving. She grabbed his arm with her good hand.

Their eyes met, and a powerful current arced between them. Desire flared again and entwined with the need sweeping through her, robbing her of her breath. When his hand lightly cupped her chin, pinpricks of awareness tingled where he touched her.

His sharply indrawn breath seemed overly loud in the stillness of the chamber. His head lowered until his lips brushed hers in a tentative kiss. He paused, pinning her with the intensity of his gaze, before capturing her lips in a searing kiss.

She felt a moan of pleasure rise up within her, but the sound could not be heard over his low growl of approval.

She felt dizzy, dazed when he lifted his lips from hers breaking the connection.

His dropped his forehead until it rested against hers. "I dinna mean to startle ye, lass," he rasped.

She wanted to tell him that he had not and gently cupped his cheek. Hoping her smile of encouragement would speak for her, she waited, watching him.

"*Och*, dinna tell me ye crave another?" he teased, obviously understanding her look.

She tilted her head back, preparing for his kiss.

This time the bone-melting kiss nearly shattered her composure. He ended the kiss, stepped back from her and stared at her as if he were seeing her for the very first time.

They were both breathing heavily when the chamber door

swung open and a deep voice boomed. "My wife wanted me to bring these linen strips to you," Garrick said to Winslow.

When neither one of them moved, he stared from one to the other. Finally he shrugged. "Do you need help wrapping her hand?" he asked, handing the linen to Winslow.

Genvieve's heart skipped a beat watching Winslow's hands fumble with the strips of cloth Garrick handed to him, before deftly wrapping her wrist. Would either man sense the jolt of awareness that rocked her every time Winslow touched her? *Mon Dieu*, she hoped they could not.

"Jillian will send Simone to sit with you tonight, Genvieve." Garrick walked to the door. "She'll be up shortly." Looking from Genvieve to Winslow and back, he shook his head and left.

Genvieve's gaze drifted to where Winslow stood awkwardly beside the bed. He almost seemed reluctant to leave. She gave him a small smile of understanding and mouthed the word, *Merci*.

With a brief nod, he turned and was gone.

Lying back against the feather-soft mattress, Genvieve let her eyes drift closed. In her mind's eye she recaptured the rough image of the Scots barbarian who was rapidly becoming her sole communicative link with the rest of the world. The potent sensuality behind his kiss reverberated through her, and she realized that he was already so much more.

Sleep beckoned, but it was the promise of dreams filled with more of Winslow's kisses that lulled her under.

Chapter Six

"Augustin," Lady Eyreka called out to her husband, drawing his attention.

When he looked over at her, his gaze deeply troubled, her heart hurt for him. "We'll find Genvieve," she said encouragingly, "I feel certain of it."

"The only evidence we have that she may have been near Merewood is her mother's cross. Though why Genvieve had it in her possession, I cannot imagine."

"Mayhap Lady Annaliese gifted it to her," Eyreka suggested hopefully.

"'Twas a gift from my grandfather to Annaliese the day she married my uncle. It is very valuable. She would never willingly part with it," he said grimly.

Eyreka lay a hand atop his where it rested on his saddle. "We'll find her."

Augustin nodded his agreement, though his eyes seemed to turn a paler shade of gray, making her wonder if he truly believed they would.

The journey back to the holding was long and arduous. Augustin's frustration at their continued failure to locate his missing cousin made him difficult to be with.

"Mayhap, husband," Eyreka coaxed, "the sight of Merewood's curtain wall will accomplish what I have not been able to."

Augustin turned at her words. "Do not speak to me in riddles, wife," he grumbled.

Eyreka sighed loudly. "Do you really think I have wits to let?"

"Nay, I—"

"You have shown your preference for the company of your own men time and again this past fortnight."

"Eyreka—"

"Do not try to soothe me with honeyed words, husband," she grumbled, highly irritated herself, and beginning to enjoy her husband's discomfort. "Had I not known better," she said lowering her voice so that only he could hear, "I would begin to doubt your claim that I alone hold your heart."

Anger flashed briefly in Augustin's eyes, changing their hue to that of winter ice, sharp and cold. "Reka," he rasped, grabbing a hold of her mount's reins and pulling her alongside of him. "That you would even question me wounds me to the quick."

The bleak look in his eyes instantly made her regret her words. She shook her head and raised her hand to cup his jaw. "Forgive me," she said softly. "I am hungry, weary, and more than ready to reach our destination. 'Tis exhaustion speaking."

Augustin nodded his head once to let her know he heard her words, but would let her suffer awhile before he would allow her to soothe his battered pride. Love for him filled her to the point where she felt certain that she would burst from it.

They rode the last few miles in silence, and it was not until they saw the guard standing at the ready, arrows notched, that either of them spoke.

"Shall I have Sara bring hot water to our chamber?" she asked, as he helped her dismount, her voice going husky with need as she pictured her soap-filled hands caressing her husband's battle-hardened body.

Their gazes met and held, understanding flashing between them, desire humming in the air. "Aye."

The hall fell silent as she made her way across the wide expanse, stopping next to the brazier to warm her tired bones. "I feel as if I have earned each of my forty summers on this last trip," Lady Eyreka moaned, holding her hands toward the flames that licked hungrily at the hunk of dried cedar. The soft scent of it hung in the air for a brief second before wafting away.

"Reka!" Lady Jillian called out from behind the buttery where she was directing one of the serving girls.

Eyreka could not help but smile at her son's wife; Jillian's answering smile was wide and filled with warmth, as the younger woman made her way over to where she stood.

"You must be exhausted," Jillian said, concern lacing her words. "Come and sit," she urged. "We have not yet supped. I'll have Gert begin to serve immediately."

Eyreka shook her head and asked, "Will you have Sara come to my chamber with hot water?"

Jillian patted Eyreka's hand and rose gracefully to do as she was bid. She paused and turned back around. "We have a guest," she said slowly.

"Do we?"

"Aye, she was badly injured," Jillian added, "and we have let her stay in the solar while she regains her strength."

"Poor woman," Eyreka sympathized. "How is it that she came to be with us?"

Jillian slowly smiled. "Winslow brought her to us ... unconscious."

"He's back, then Roderick—"

"Winslow came alone."

Eyreka knew there was more to the tale and it would have to wait. "Tell me about our guest."

Jillian nodded, "Her throat was injured, and the poor thing cannot speak."

"Does she have a name?" Eyreka wanted to know.

"Aye, 'tis—"

"Eyreka!" Augustin's voice bellowed across the chamber, his patience obviously at an end from waiting for his promised bath and more.

She placed a hand to Jillian's forearm. "You must excuse my husband; he is over-tired. You can tell me more later."

Jillian smiled knowingly. "And in need of your soothing touch," she said in a low voice so that only Eyreka could hear her.

Eyreka nodded and hurried over to join her husband.

"Did you tell her about Genvieve?" Garrick asked, joining his wife.

"Not the whole of it—" she began.

"Obviously de Chauret has other more pressing needs to be seen to than visiting our wounded guest," he said, raising his eyebrows suggestively.

"Walk with me," Jillian suggested. "It is early yet, and the air still holds its warmth."

Garrick reached out and placed her arm through his. Leading her across the hall to the side door, they walked outside into the night.

⇶⇷

SIMONE LEFT THE tray laden with the evening's meal on the table next to Genvieve. "The lord of the keep has returned," the young woman said, making conversation, though she knew Genvieve could not respond.

"Such a handsome man," she continued, straightening the bed linens and coming to stand beside the bed. "He's a Norman baron," Simone finished.

Norman. Genvieve's mind grasped that tidbit of information and started to whirl with questions. She remembered being told they were at Merewood Keep, but could not remember why the name was so familiar. She racked her brain trying to uncover the reason while Simone continued to fuss, trying to help her eat.

The sudden wish that Winslow was here helping her eat made her jaw still in the act of chewing. Genvieve remembered the feel of his fingertips brushing against her lips as he fed her. Moisture pooled in her mouth, and she swallowed without thinking, and instantly started to choke on the half-chewed bit of venison stew.

Simone whacking her between the shoulder blades was more a hindrance than help. Finally, after a few tense moments, when she thought she'd choke to death, the offending bit of meat was dislodged, and she could draw a breath once again.

"Are you all right?" Simone asked, worry creasing her brow.

Genvieve opened her mouth to speak, then chastised herself for trying to tax her aching throat. The bout of coughing hurt like the very devil. She clamped her jaw tightly closed and nodded.

Simone seemed satisfied that Genvieve would not succumb to anymore fits of choking and continued with her monologue. "Lord A—"

Her words were cut off by her name being called from just beyond the open doorway.

"I almost forgot I've got to help with the bath water!" With a shake of her head, Simone hurried out of the chamber, leaving Genvieve to wonder about the Norman lord of the keep.

Chapter Seven

MacInness felt as if he had been bludgeoned with a cudgel on both sides of his head. He shook his head to clear it and descended the steps to the hall. Instead of following his own advice and maintaining distance between himself and the lovely Genvieve, he was drawn to her, spending his free time with her.

As it happened every time he left her presence, the further he walked away from Genvieve, the clearer his thoughts became. By the time he crossed the wide expanse of the hall, he was able to rationalize his reaction to the disturbing woman. Not that he normally spent an inordinate amount of time thinking about any woman. He felt responsible for her. The same way he felt for his sisters, Bronwyn and Moira. He descended the steps and walked outside.

Aye, he thought, making his way to the stables. Think of her as a sister.

Losing himself in the task of caring for his horse, he was surprised when Garrick called out to him. "MacInness!"

He had just finished currying his new mount. He had still not forgiven the Norman infidels for shooting his four-footed friend Duncan between the eyes with an arrow. He emerged from the dimly lit stable into the bright afternoon.

Looking about him, he finally noticed his friend standing atop the raised wooden platform that ran the length of the curtain wall surrounding the entire holding. He walked over and started up the steps.

"Have you met him?" Garrick asked, before he reached the top step.

"Who?" MacInness countered.

"De Chauret," Garrick answered. "The new Lord of the Merewood Keep."

MacInness shook his head, "Nay. I've been busy in the stables, tending the new mount ye've let me use. I've yet to thank ye properly."

"I am sorry that you lost Duncan," Garrick said quietly.

"I helped him to take his first steps right after he'd been born."

Garrick nodded.

"I trained him. We'd been through countless battles together, I—"

"'Tis not wrong for a man to admit he misses his horse," Garrick said, a small smile tipping the corner of his mouth upward.

"'Tis no' just that," MacInness said slowly. "I've got ta train another bloody mount now," he said to hide the hurt.

Garrick waited, but MacInness didn't want to admit, even to his friend, just how much he'd loved that horse. Duncan had saved his life on more than one occasion. They were a team, unbeatable in battle.

"...should be in the hall..." Garrick was saying.

"I dinna hear ye," MacInness said, realizing that his friend had been speaking to him while he was woolgathering.

Garrick's brow creased and MacInness could feel the waves of irritation rolling off the other warrior. "I said, de Chauret will be in the hall for the evening meal. Join me, I'll introduce you."

MacInness started to mumble that he had no use for Norman dogs, but caught himself before he insulted the new lord of the keep.

The sound of voices raised in celebration reached them as

they entered the brightly lit hall. Lady Eyreka motioned for them to join her at the table on the raised dais. MacInness followed his friend, his hackles beginning to rise at the sight of so many Norman warriors surrounding Garrick's mother. Just then, the giant of a man sitting next to her leaned over and whispered something in her ear, making her laugh softly.

Four of the Norman guard surrounding his friend's mother smiled. She laughed again. MacInness could not believe what he was seeing. They smiled again. Mayhap he'd have to hold back his judgment of these men until later.

"Garrick." The huge warrior rose to his feet, extending his hand.

"Augustin," Garrick said smiling, reaching out to grasp the older man's hand.

The man standing beside Lady Eyreka glanced at MacInness, and he could feel the warrior's questioning gaze settle on him, but remained silent as he walked around the table to join them where they stood.

"My vassal, Winslow MacInness," Garrick said.

MacInness nodded his head toward Augustin.

"Augustin de Chauret, Lord of Merewood Keep," Garrick added, without a change in the inflection of his voice. MacInness could detect no rancor here. His friend seemed to have accepted his removal as lord. He'd have to consider this later. That his friend would act as seneschal now instead of lord bothered him. Why didn't it seem to have an effect on Garrick?

MacInness studied the older man before him. His dark hair was streaked with gray, but he was heavily muscled, making him wonder if the man was not younger than he first thought. He noticed then that the man was almost as tall as himself. He smiled.

"You will find MacInness is a man of few words," Garrick was saying.

"A trait I would gladly live with," Augustin answered affably, letting his gaze slip away from MacInness and come to rest on the young blond-headed knight who had bent down to speak to Lady Eyreka.

MacInness noticed that Lady Eyreka was smiling, and de Chauret was frowning. So, the new Lord of Merewood did not like his wife smiling at the younger, handsome warrior. MacInness grudgingly admitted that alone was reason to reevaluate his opinion of the Norman Baron. The man obviously cared for Lady Eyreka.

MacInness shifted his attention back to the men still speaking to him, but made an unconscious promise to watch the young Norman warrior. He did not give his trust easily where family was concerned, and Lady Eyreka treated him as if he were her own son. He could do no less than to protect her as if he truly were.

"—stayed for the execution?" Garrick was asking de Chauret.

The older warrior nodded. "While I have no liking for the deed, it serves as a reminder to those who would strike out against king and country."

"Whose neck did they stretch before spilling the mon's innards and lopping off his head?" MacInness was sorry to have missed the traitor's name.

"Owen of Sedgeworth," Garrick answered, his jaw tight with emotion.

MacInness felt a sense of rightness settle over him. Justice was sweet, though revenge would have tasted sweeter than Merewood's legendary mead. His thoughts turned toward the woman he still cared for. Sedgeworth had tried to have Lady Jillian killed, more than once. The pain she suffered while living under the man's roof was reason enough to have the man drawn and quartered. He smiled remembering his own offer to strip the man's skin from his sorry hide. He would have relished slowly killing the man.

"The king had to make an example of Sedgeworth," de Chauret was saying. "No one can hold back revenues or try to side with the rebels against King William and expect to live to tell of it," he finished.

MacInness let his gaze meet Garrick's. He could feel the violent need within his friend, churning just below the calm surface of Garrick's stance. He too felt the blood begin to pound through his veins remembering all that Lady Jillian had suffered. Hatred was an emotion they had both learned to harness as long as they didn't hold it in too long. He knew his friend would welcome a physical outlet—sparring. As in the past, all he would have to do is suggest the place and he knew Garrick would meet him there.

"Lower bailey?" he quietly asked, hoping his friend would be willing to cross swords with him.

Garrick nodded his head.

"'Twill be dark soon," de Chauret said, though his unasked question of why hung in the air between the men.

"Yer welcome to join us," MacInness offered.

De Chauret slowly nodded and flashed a thin smile in his lady wife's general direction, before following the men outside.

⟫⟩⟨⟪

JILLIAN AND EYREKA hurried through the side door and around the rear of the building.

Though quiet at first, with only the sound of the booted feet of the guards patrolling the raised platform echoing in the late afternoon air, a faint clanging of steel against steel rose above the trill of a night bird and the rush of the wind. Jillian tugged on Eyreka's arm as they followed the sound to the lower bailey, stopping far enough away from the men so as not to be seen. There was no danger of being heard above the din of hand-to-hand combat.

MacInness's claymore flashed for a moment, poised to strike. But Garrick's broadsword sliced through the air to meet the deadly blow. The two men muttered curses at one another, grunting under the force of the blows they rained upon one another, while de Chauret stood back, a broad grin on his face.

"Why are they fighting?" Jillian whispered.

"Releasing pent-up anger," Eyreka said. "Owen of Sedgeworth was executed while we were in London."

She watched her son's wife closely, but still almost missed the flash of emotion that swept across the younger woman's features. Eyreka recognized it as a mix of pain and anger, and silently praised Jillian for her strength. Jillian stood just a bit straighter, drew in a breath and nodded. "He was foolish enough to think his crimes would go unnoticed."

Eyreka nodded her agreement. "Augustin wanted to kill Owen once he learned what that evil man had done to you."

"Anger not released festers away unseen. 'Tis best to get it out, rather than let it destroy you. My husband is a complex man," she said solemnly. "He and Winslow feel responsible for what I suffered, though neither of them were there through the worst of it."

Eyreka grabbed Jillian's hand and held fast. She could feel the younger woman's pain, wanting to help, but not willing to bring up the past and all its demons. It was a past that they shared, and a good man's death that they held themselves responsible for, though some would say otherwise.

Eyreka could feel the tension building within Jillian. She had not wanted to be the one to tell her that her former guardian, the man who had taken her into his home not as a magnanimous gesture, but to serve his own ends, had had to pay the piper. Jillian had suffered more than Eyreka would have thought possible, while living at Sedgeworth Keep, but she had an inner core of pure steel. Owen's wife had not been able to break her spirit. Jillian's body may be scarred, but her giving soul had not succumbed to the beatings.

The sudden absence of sound alerted Eyreka to the fact that the men had stopped. When she turned her head, she noticed the three men stood staring at them. She wrapped her arm around Jillian and started to move away.

"Nay," MacInness said, stopping their flight with one word. "Dinna go."

The sweat dripped down the sides of the tall Scot's face and as she watched, he swiped at it with his arm. Her son and her husband each took a step toward them and stopped. She could feel Jillian trembling.

Garrick's voice was rough with emotion when he finally spoke. "I would have told you later."

Jillian nodded. Eyreka pulled her closer; trying to suffuse some of her own strength into Jillian, hoping it would help.

Augustin looked to Eyreka and then let his troubled gaze slide over to the shaking woman. "'Tis done." He gently cupped the side of Jillian's face. "Best to put it behind you," he said softly, reaching up with his thumb to catch a tear.

Eyreka's heart swelled with love for Augustin, another man would not have cared. But her husband was not just any other man. When the fates had decided to bless her with the love of a lifetime for the second time, they could not have chosen a better man.

⇉⇇

MACINNESS DECIDED TO like the man. The Norman did not have to care enough about Garrick's wife to try to soothe her feelings, but the man did. He would definitely have to take the time to discover more about the new lord of the keep. Though he did not like the looks of the man's personal guard, and did not trust Normans as a rule, he would make an exception in de Chauret's case.

Chapter Eight

"Genvieve?" de Chauret rasped. "Did you say our injured guest's name is Genvieve?"

Garrick straightened, but did not back up a pace. He held his ground. "Aye."

"What does she look like?" de Chauret demanded in low tones, the edge of his temper taking on a life of its own ... a living, breathing entity.

"Dark hair, gray eyes." Garrick said, pausing to consider. "She was bruised and battered when MacInness brought her here, but now—"

"*Mon Dieu,*" de Chauret ground out, raking a hand through his gray-streaked hair. "Eyreka!" he bellowed, striding across the hall, anger punctuating his footsteps. The sharp sound of his heavy footfall against the dry planked boards echoed in the silence.

He could feel his wife's presence just a few paces behind him, hurrying to catch up with him; the connection was always thus for them. He gritted his teeth together as he mounted the steps, taking them two at a time. "She's here," he said over his shoulder.

"She who?" Eyreka asked breathlessly.

"Genvieve," he said simply, yanking the solar door open. Relief flooded through him, threatening to rob his legs of their strength. His young cousin sat in a chair next to the arrowslit, plying her needle through a bit of linen.

Her sharp intake of breath told him she was shocked to see him. How was it that she did not know he would be here? Merewood was his, why would she be surprised to see him?

As he watched, the expression on her face changed from bored disinterest to disbelief. She opened her mouth to speak, but stopped and put a hand to her throat. The raspy sound that emerged stopped him in his tracks.

⋙⋘

GENVIEVE'S EYES FILLED with tears at the sight of her handsome cousin filling the chamber doorway. His powerful build always reminded her of their grandfather. Shoulders broad enough to hold the weight of the world upon them. She blinked away the tears, now was not the time.

"We thought you lost to us," he said, his voice suspiciously husky.

I'm found, she thought. The words ringing loud and clear in her head. She started to move her mouth to speak, the need was so strong, but would not embarrass herself further by making any more wounded animal sounds. She had overheard one of the maids use that very expression when speaking of her just last eve. The realization that words could cut one to the quick and leave one bleeding had not been lost on her.

One moment he was standing, hands fisted at his sides, the next he was pulling her into his embrace, squeezing the breath right out of her.

"But how did you find your way here?" he asked finally, letting her sit down, but still holding her hand in both of his.

She looked down at those hands. The backs were as scarred as she remembered. She ran the tip of her forefinger across the c-shaped scar on his right hand. She looked up and found him staring at her.

"I still remember how badly you wounded my young pride that day."

She nodded. Bringing his hand closer, she pressed her lips against the scar and laid his hand against her cheek. They had been so young. Augustin twelve summers and she just six. She had not meant to swing the dagger, but her cousin had surprised her by jumping out from behind the stand of evergreens at the back of their grandparents' garden at Rouen.

Instinct had her slashing out with the blade. Fate had it connecting with the flesh on the back of Augustin's hand. She still remembered the blood. It had been everywhere. She could still feel the roiling in her gut and the surge of bile that sped up her throat. But Augustin had needed her; he grabbed hold of her sleeve and clamped it on top of the jagged wound.

Through her tears, she saw the color leach from his face. It was then she realized that she must not throw up. Her favorite cousin needed her. After all, it was her fault he was standing there, bleeding all over their grandmother's cinder path. She nodded, though he had not spoken, and pulled the threads from the shoulder of her bliaut, letting the sleeve slide down her arm. Wadding it against the wound, as she had seen her own mother do when poor Marie had sliced her finger instead of the fresh-baked bread, she prayed as she put pressure on the awful gash.

"I see some things shall remain forever in our minds, cousin," Augustin said gently.

She had suffered from pangs of guilt long after the threads that held his young flesh together were removed. It had healed quickly, but the unusual shape of the scar would remain forever.

Winslow found me, she mouthed, though he shook his head, not understanding. She tried again, pleading with her cousin to watch her lips closely, so he could try to read the movements of her mouth. *I did not know where he was taking me.*

He averted his eyes, as if the very thought of her not being able to speak was painful to him. She gently touched his sleeve. When his eyes met hers, she could see the answer to her next question. He would need time before he could accept her crippling problem. *Did he fear the worst, too, that the affliction would be permanent?*

"I thought I heard voices, comin' from yer room, lass," Winslow's voice carried across the room to them, sounding low and soothing.

Genvieve's heart seemed to skip a beat, and the room grew suddenly warm. She placed a hand to her breast, watched his eyes follow her movement.

"'Twas a surprise to me as well," Winslow said walking toward her. The weight of his step crushed the bits of rosemary and thyme that Lady Eyreka and Lady Jillian religiously sprinkled about the rushes. Freed, the clean scent swirled upward, mixing with the mid-morning breeze wafting toward her from the arrowslit.

Augustin turned toward MacInness and cocked his head to one side. "My cousin did not speak. How is it that you can answer unuttered questions?"

MacInness stopped in his tracks and glanced first to his overlord, then Genvieve. "When the lass is surprised, she always raises a hand to her breast."

Augustin took a step closer to the tall Scot. Genvieve could feel the waves of tension filling the air around them. She did not want Augustin to be angry with Winslow. He was her friend, her rescuer, the only one who seemed to be able to understand what she desperately needed to say.

One look at Augustin confirmed that he was rapidly losing the hold on his temper. The set of his jaw and the way his hands fisted behind his back were indications he was just short of bellowing. She loved Augustin, but really had no time for one of his outbursts now.

She leapt to her feet and stood right in front of him, placing a hand to his chest. Tilting her head back, she waited until her cousin looked down at her. His jaw was still clenched, but his eyes had lost the lethal stare he had tried to level Winslow with.

"Genvieve?" Though but one word, his meaning was not lost on her. She knew he was only trying to protect her as he had so many times in their youth. He acted more the role of older brother than cousin. It was time to remind him that she didn't need his help where the tall Scots warrior was concerned.

Her heart clenched in her breast. Winslow had slipped into the role of protector from the start. Warmth crept up her neck; she could feel it staining her cheeks, as if she had stood too close to a brightly burning fire.

She mouthed the words, *I am all right*, willing Augustin to understand, but she could see his confusion. Not knowing what else to do, she turned to face Winslow. She mouthed the words, *I am all right*.

MacInness placed a hand to her shoulder and nodded his head. "I think the lass is trying to tell ye she's safe with me," he said in a gruff voice.

Genvieve waited one heartbeat, then another, before dropping her hands to her sides and taking a step back away from the seemingly calmer men. She whispered a quick prayer of thanks to her Maker and sat back down.

As she watched, Augustin clenched his jaw and inhaled a deep breath. His massive chest expanded with it. He fisted his hands, twice, then ran a hand through his hair impatiently. "Why should I believe that she feels safe with you?" he demanded, his voice raspy.

"Ask the lass herself," MacInness said in calm even tones.

Genvieve laid a hand on MacInness's arm and smiled up at him, before turning to her cousin and nodding.

Augustin raked his hands through his hair again then turned and headed for the door. Leaning against the door jam, he bellowed, "Georges!"

Genvieve wondered what Augustin would want with their cousin, Georges.

He is a warrior of great skill, she thought. *Mayhap he means to challenge Winslow.*

Her eyes darted over to where the tall redheaded warrior stood, feet apart, arms folded over his massive chest. He did not seem worried. Nay, she thought, he looked very relaxed. 'Twas his easy manner that helped her to calm down while waiting for Georges to arrive.

"Genvieve?" Georges's shock was palpable. "You are well?" He walked over to where she sat.

She nodded.

He glanced at Augustin then back. "You were never so silent before," he said, watching her closely. "What happened to you? We've been searching for you."

Augustin answered, "MacInness found her, but not before she'd been injured." He paused, then added, "She cannot speak."

The shocked expression on Georges's face was not unexpected, nor was his next question. "Will she heal?"

Winslow spoke up, "Aye, she will."

His absolute surety of that fact brought tears to her eyes. She blinked them away.

"Georges, I need you to take a company of men and ride to London," Augustin said. "I need you to deliver a missive to my uncle, with all haste."

With one last look at her, Georges nodded. "We should be ready to leave within the hour."

Augustin nodded his agreement and watched the warrior stride purposefully from the room before he turned his penetrating gaze upon Genvieve's self-proclaimed protector.

Lady Eyreka had been quiet through the entire exchange of words between the two warriors; she must have decided she had waited long enough. Genvieve watched her walk toward Winslow.

"Thank you seems so little, Winslow," Lady Eyreka said, a small smile gracing her fine-boned features, "when compared to the result of your actions."

She holds herself like a queen, Genvieve noted. Her bearing is so royal.

While she watched, Lady Eyreka took one of Winslow's massive hands in her own and squeezed it. He shifted from one foot to the other, oddly disconcerted by her show of affection. As Genvieve watched the by-play, she realized the true reason for Winslow's reaction. Lady Eyreka pulled the warrior closer, stood up on the tips of her toes and brushed a kiss on his cheek.

Genvieve's gaze slid over to where her cousin stood, rigid as an ancient cairn of stones marking a battle site.

"Reka," Winslow began, backing away from her embrace.

"Lady Eyreka," Augustin bit out.

"I have given him leave to address me thusly," she chastised him. "Winslow and I have long been acquainted, husband," she said smiling warmly. "Lady Jillian and I owe him our lives."

"How is it that I have heard this said on more than one occasion to more than one of your son's guard?" Augustin demanded. Genvieve recognized all the signs of his temper starting to simmer, knowing that it lay just beneath the calm surface he allowed the rest of the world to see.

Winslow threw back his head and laughed aloud. Genvieve wrapped her arms around herself and shut her eyes tightly, waiting for her cousin's temper to erupt. After a few moments of utter silence, she heard the loud intake of breath. She opened one eye, hoping that somehow the inevitable had been avoided.

To her shock, her cousin had moved to stand by his wife and had his arm wrapped about her. His facial expression was still thunderous, but he had relaxed his battle stance.

"You will tell me later, wife," she heard Augustin say.

Her cousin no longer allowed his temper to get the better of him. Augustin had changed since the last time she'd seen him. When had this happened? She looked over at the couple and saw the look that they exchanged. It spoke volumes; they communicated without words, a single look and each had understood the other.

A bone-deep sorrow swept through her, leaving her weak. Francois and she had been able to speak without the need for words. A look, a touch, a mere twist of the lips, had been far more effective than words. An uncomfortable edginess accompanied her sad thoughts. She missed him, after three long and lonely years, she still ached for his touch, still reached for him in the darkness.

And yes, she thought bleakly, *she still loved him*. What she felt for Winslow was not love, could not be love... it was need pure and simple.

Genvieve had hoped to be able to put the past behind her and move forward with the arrangement of her second marriage to Guy du Lacque. But Guy had given his life for the Norman cause during the Saxon Uprisings that swept through Northumbria. She was not one who usually dwelt on the past, but hers had been happy ... but for the lost babes.

The fact that her cousin had managed to pull his life together, and in fact had found someone to love again, disturbed Genvieve. She did not know if she were capable of taking the chance of loving someone...and losing them. The cost outweighed the gain. She would never love, or marry again.

"I think Genvieve needs to rest," Lady Eyreka announced to those still crowded in the chamber.

With a pointed look, they left, one by one. All except for Winslow who glared at the lady of the keep. "I dinna think ye mean to boot me out as well."

Genvieve wished she could ask Winslow to stay with her, but was afraid to strain her throat. She slowly stood and walked toward him. The expression on his face was guarded and she could not guess his thoughts. Mayhap that was a good thing, considering his bone melting kisses.

"Lady Eyreka," Winslow began, but before he could finish the older woman nodded. She glanced at Genvieve as she crossed the room, then swept through the door, closing it behind her.

"Dinna be surprised," Winslow said as if reading her mind.

Was her every thought plastered on her face for all to see? A whisper of a memory speared through her head. *You're right to fear us, wench!* The voice in her head had a shiver racing up her spine, remembering her captor's words.

"You've naught to fear, lass," Winslow whispered, taking her in his arms. "I promised not to hurt ye, and I mean ta honor that promise."

Instead of kissing the breath out of her as she hoped, he pressed his lips to her forehead and slid a hand up her back and into her hair. With a deft movement, he eased her head onto his shoulder where she fit perfectly.

The heat pouring off of him eased the tension and fear that threatened to overwhelm her. She sighed and turned her head to press her lips to his collarbone.

He jolted at her touch, but when she looked up at him, his mouth was grim and she wondered if it had been something else that caused the movement.

"'Tis only right that ye'll be with yer family soon, lass." He dropped his hands and took a step back. "I must get back to my duties."

Was he saying goodbye? No, she reasoned. It would be at least a fortnight before Georges reached London and could make the trip back. Winslow wouldn't leave before then, would he? She stepped forward and his eyes narrowed.

"I've work."

She reached out a hand to him and instead of the reaction she expected, he stood his ground and waited. Genvieve couldn't stop herself from brushing her hand across the strong line of his jaw. Her heart tumbled in her breast, such a handsome face.

Her Scotsman shivered at her touch. Ah, she thought, his body tells the truth. A glance at his tortured expression and she had the answer she sought. What she would do with the answer, she had no idea.

"I've—"

Work, she mouthed, rising to her toes and pressing her lips to his.

Winslow's arms wrapped around her and pulled her close,

right where she wanted to be. She tilted her head back to look up at him, and her heart began to pound in her breast. Desire warred with the agony etched on his handsome face.

He lowered his mouth toward hers then paused, as if waiting for permission. She reached up and grabbed him by the hair. His lips captured hers in a kiss that demanded her full attention. Warm firm lips molded hers, drawing feelings she'd buried back to life.

An ache blossomed in her belly, spreading upward toward her heart. He slid a hand down her spine, until he cupped her backside and pressed her intimately against him.

His kiss deepened as his tongue took possession of her, boldly tangling then withdrawing, making her moan with need.

Pinned against him, awareness mingled with shock. His warrior's body tensed, and the part of him nestled against her body grew rock hard and began to pulse. Her body hungered and her heart ached. She ignored her heart and arched her back.

He broke the kiss and dipped low tracing her collarbone with his tongue. Need screamed through her as her sleeping gown slid off her shoulder and his head dipped lower. He latched onto her breast as if he'd die without the sustenance only she could offer.

He switched to her other breast, his hands still gripping her backside. His tongue traced a circle around her nipple, teasing her, tempting her with tiny licks and flicks of his tongue that had her whimpering with need.

His head shot up and his look of desire changed to one of shock. "I'm sorry, lass," he rasped. "I didna mean—"

To kiss me?

His eyes widened, reacting to the movement of her lips, understanding perfectly.

A heady feeling filled her, and she dared to ask, *To make me want you?*

But his reaction was not what she anticipated. His eyes narrowed.

She turned away, bereft. He'd made her ache for fulfillment

and now he drew back from her, withholding what her body craved. She was no maid to be teased and left wanting. She knew the paradise that could be theirs if Winslow hadn't stopped. But how could she tell him?

He placed his hands on her shoulders. The weight of those hands reminded her of how they felt cupping her backside, kneading the fullness of her bottom as if he enjoyed what she'd always thought was too fleshy.

She wanted to ask him why he stopped, but sensed he wouldn't answer. He dropped his hands, and she turned around in time to see the back of him as he walked out the door.

"Winslow?" her words came out as a garbled rasp.

He stopped and looked over his shoulder. "I'm sorry, lass."

CHAPTER NINE

GENVIEVE SPENT THE next few days wondering why Winslow hadn't been by to see her, hoping it wasn't because he regretted the passion that still had the power to make her tremble.

Jillian and Eyreka took turns visiting her, distracting her, until both proclaimed she was recovered enough to get out of bed.

Today would be the first time she'd left her chamber since the night desperation had her trying to run away.

"You look lovely," Jillian proclaimed stepping back to admire her handiwork. "The dark blue bliaut suits you."

It was just the three of them in the chamber, so Genvieve risked trying to use her voice. Her thank you came out as a barely intelligible broken sound.

Jillian grabbed her hand and squeezed it. "Don't push yourself," she soothed. "Your voice will return. It's getting stronger."

Eyreka moved to stand by Genvieve's side. Reaching up, the other woman brushed a strand of hair from Genvieve's eyes. "Mayhap it would be wise to try to speak," Eyreka said. "At least a few words each day."

Genvieve shook her head.

"Why not?"

Eyreka was watching her closely, but Genvieve refused to tell her about the comments she'd overheard one of the serving women make about her attempts to speak. She shrugged in answer.

Jillian's gaze narrowed and Genvieve patted her throat. Her sign that it hurt to speak.

Garrick's wife's expression immediately changed. "Reka, she shouldn't rush to use her voice if it still pains her."

Genvieve hated lying, but it was necessary. She'd not be ridiculed by her cousin's serving women or the people in his holding. Everything was too new. Her cousin didn't need the added worry of chastising his people for speaking their mind, even if their words flayed her to the bone.

"Well, then," Eyreka said. "We've a lot of duties to accomplish today, beginning with the food stores."

The morning passed while the women counted barrels of flour, salted meat, and mead. Immersed in familiar tasks, Genvieve felt needed. When it was time for their nooning meal, Genvieve was weary, but not ready to seek her chamber and rest. She'd spent far too much time in her chamber.

"Angelique will help us sort through the linens and see what needs to be mended or replaced." Eyreka's announcement had her wondering where her younger cousin had been spending her time. Genvieve had only seen her a few times and only in passing.

She reached over and placed her hand on Eyreka's. The lady of the keep set her goblet of watered wine down and looked at her.

Why? Genvieve mouthed slowly so Eyreka would understand.

"Angelique has been very busy with lessons." The older woman smiled. "She's learning how to manage a holding of this size, but also how to record what stores we have."

Jillian nodded. "She's very bright and willing to do anything her new mother asks."

Eyreka's eyes filled, and Genvieve wondered why. She squeezed Eyreka's hand and let go.

"She learned how to care for the sick and wounded of her

father's people," Jillian said. "And kept her stepmother, my mother-in-law, from bleeding to death when that madman's sword—"

"Jillian, please."

Genvieve wondered what the lady of the keep didn't want her to know. But the struggle to speak was still too much of a barrier, and in the end, she forced herself to look away from the pain-filled expression on Jillian's face and resume eating.

There was much to be done.

"Genvieve!" Angelique darted into the room and into her arms.

"*Ma petite,*" she rasped, her voice a jagged sound in the quiet of the room.

"Then it's true?" Angelique pulled out of her arms, a look of horror on her face.

Genvieve nodded, unwilling to utter another word while her young cousin stared at her as if she'd crawled out from under a rock.

But the little one's tears caught her off guard. "Does it pain you terribly?"

Genvieve shook her head.

"Won't you please talk to me?" Angelique had grabbed a hold of Genvieve's hand and was tugging on it.

Love for her cousin swamped her. She'd worried about Angelique's adjustment to life when her father married after all of his years of widowhood, but could see from the way Angelique spoke and acted that she was secure in her new life.

"Soon, *ma petite*," she said, her voice grating though the now quiet room.

"I'm very busy these days," Angelique confided, looking over at Jillian and Eyreka, "but I don't mind the endless duties."

"Much," the other women added, smiling at the little girl. Angelique looked sheepish as she grinned at Genvieve.

At least Genvieve could stop worrying about Angelique. It was clear the little one was delighted with her new mother and her new life.

"About those linens," Lady Eyreka said gently.

GEORGES WAS DUE to return any day and Genvieve wanted to be there when he delivered her father's missive. Had her mother fully recovered from whatever illness prompted her to send for Genvieve, interrupting her journey north, taking her away from Angelique?

A fortnight had passed with her slipping seamlessly into the day-to-day tasks involved maintaining the keep. While she worked, her thoughts drifted toward a certain Scotsman, his absence burning a hole in her new life.

At night she dreamt of Francois and her miscarried babies. During the day, while her hands were busy, her mind and traitorous body inevitably focused on Winslow's devastating kisses.

Thoughts of him muddled her mind and she'd lost her place counting their store of foodstuffs more times than she'd like to admit. Since she couldn't speak, no one questioned how long it took her to record her numbers on the growing list of Merewood's inventory.

Hurrying across the lower bailey on her way to fetch newly sharpened eating daggers from the blacksmith, she caught a glimpse of Winslow speaking to one of the serving women and smiling down at her.

His name on her lips had her drawing the hurt inside and clamping them shut tight. He was speaking to the woman who'd made her voice the object of many a jest. Genvieve watched the way the woman brushed a strand of flaxen hair over her shoulder and wondered how the woman would look without her hair.

Jealousy clawed at her belly, making it ache. Did he mean so much to her or was it simply his lack of attention and loss of his friendship?

So, he was still here...and avoiding her. The kisses they shared had not meant anything to him. Needing to sort through her feelings she turned away and sought out the blacksmith. There was work to be done and duties to see to before she could escape to her chamber.

"Genvieve?"

She hastened her steps, ignoring Winslow. He'd not noticed her before when he was smiling at the pasty-faced Saxon wench, so she pretended not to hear him now.

"MacInness!"

Augustin. She looked over her shoulder in time to see the confusion furrowing Winslow's brow. As he turned to answer the summons, her heart sank. She'd more than grown accustomed to the man's company and friendship. But what she felt for the Scots mercenary couldn't be more than unfulfilled desire. Could it?

In her haste to fetch the daggers and return to her chamber, she'd managed to trip on her hem and tear her bliaut. Now she'd have to change for the evening meal.

Her stomach rumbled as she hastened to wash and dress. A glance out the arrowslit told her that she'd have to hurry. A light breeze blew in and carried with it the scent of freshly baked bread. Preparations for the evening meal would no doubt be underway. Having worked with Lady Jillian and Lady Eyreka, she knew the kitchen would be bustling with activity.

Spurred on by her hunger, Genvieve ventured from the solar downward. Her booted feet made little sound as she descended to the hall below. Raucous sounds grew louder with each step she took. The deep timbre of her cousin's voice reached her ears as she paused in the doorway to the hall.

"I wilna wed." She recognized the depth and tone as Winslow's voice, though it had a harshness she had not heard before.

"You cannot ignore a missive from the king," she heard Augustin reply.

"I dinna even know the lass." Winslow said again.

"Genvieve will be a good wife, she has healing hands, a kind heart, and pleasant demeanor," Augustin said convincingly. But Genvieve had not heard past the mention of her name and the words—good wife. She shook her head, denying that she had even heard her name mentioned. There must be another woman by the same name living within these walls. Augustin could not be speaking of her. She had her father's word that she would never have to wed again.

She heard her name mentioned a second time and burst into the hall. Forgotten were all of the years of training to be a lady; all that mattered was her need to act. Anger punctuated each step she took, bringing her closer to the two who thought to take control of her life. *Mon Dieu*, she would never let that happen again.

The strained scratchy sound that she made caught the attention of the men she strode toward. "I'll never marry again," she said, but her words were lost in the garbled sound that reminded her of her inability to speak and her dependence on the kindness of others.

Her gaze locked onto the broad and powerful form of the only person who cared enough to take the time to even try to understand her. Winslow's stance was eerily familiar. A chill raced up her spine, as she tried to remember why it was so.

"Genvieve," Augustin called to her, reaching out to take her by the arm.

Her gaze darted back and forth between both men. How could she make them understand? How could she convey her wish? Did they not know of her father's last agreement with her? Aimory de Chauret had given his word, promised she'd not have to wed again.

"I'm glad you are here," Augustin said in a low voice, guiding her to a bench by the far wall. "We have much to discuss," he said cryptically, neither confirming nor denying what she feared.

"The lass has a right to know," Winslow ground out, as he stalked over to where she sat.

She nodded her emphatic agreement and cleared her throat to tell the men how she felt. It hurt to speak, but she needed them to hear her refusal. "More right than either of you have to plan my life."

Winslow's frown was fierce, but she didn't know if he agreed with her or not.

Augustin's gaze turned bleak as it always did when she mouthed words to him, or tried to control the scratchy, freakish sound of her voice. He looked away, motioning to one of the serving girls. She carried a tray with a pitcher and four goblets over to the table. The girl started to pour, but he waved her away. With a bob, she turned and hastily fled the hall.

The sound of soft footfalls rustling the rushes strewn across the floor caught Genvieve's attention. Genvieve looked up and saw Eyreka walking purposefully toward their small group.

Will she help me, and with me against her own husband?

"Genvieve," Eyreka reached out to grasp her hands, squeezing them briefly before letting go. She turned toward her husband. "Have you told her?"

"Nay." He glanced at Genvieve out of the corner of his eye. "But I think it safe to assume she knows."

"*Bollocks!*" Winslow's curse echoed her thoughts. "The lass doesna *ken* what she is expected to do." Winslow's gaze locked with hers.

Genvieve suppressed the sudden urge to fling her arms about him. She stared at him and waited for him to tell her, needing to hear the words from his lips.

Augustin cleared his throat. "Georges returned earlier." He paused and looked from Winslow to her. "I have had an answer from your father," he began, only to pause to pour out four mugs of mead.

"Get it said," Winslow urged.

Genvieve nodded her agreement, accepting the mug placed in her hands, praying that she somehow had misunderstood what she overheard.

"Your father is greatly relieved to hear of your safe return," Augustin began, "but was fraught with worry over the kidnapping."

Genvieve fought the urge to speak, it was pointless when only Winslow took the time or made the effort to understand her. Even if she could utter the words, she still had no memory of what had happened.

Augustin paused and looked at Eyreka. She smiled at him and nodded, a silent entreaty to continue.

"It is the issue of your safety that has convinced the baron to change his mind," her cousin said, slowly staring at her.

Genvieve could feel the numbness start to creep up her legs. Nay. Papa would never go back on his word.

She looked frantically from one face to another. Her cousin looked away, but Winslow held her questioning gaze. Eyreka leaned closer, reaching out a hand, and took hold of Genvieve's chilled fingers. The warmth was meant to soothe, but the numbness had reached her roiling stomach, accompanied by an icy feeling of shock.

Her own father had betrayed her trust. He knew how she suffered when her babes had been taken from her…when Francois had died…and then her betrothed, Guy…

Unaware that anyone addressed her, she felt the gentle touch on her brow.

"You have to," she heard through the haze that seemed to rise from the rush-strewn floor.

"I can't," she said, though it was barely above a garbled whisper, and no one seemed to be paying attention to her.

"I canna," she heard Winslow answer the command.

Genvieve wanted to thank Winslow for refusing to do as he was bid, without knowing or caring why he refused her hand. It would be easier for him to accept her refusal.

Strong hands gripped her upper arms, and a welcoming heat suffused her cold, clammy body. The mist evaporated, and she realized she had been helped to her feet and was standing before the man who saved her life, the man who cared enough to interpret her unspoken words for more than a fortnight now. The man who boldly refused her father's offer of her hand in marriage.

"Ye must *ken* what I say, lass," Winslow said in a harsh voice, his grip tightening around her arms.

She stared up at him and was again surprised by the emotion that rose from within her. His amber gaze seemed tortured. She nodded and mouthed the words, *I'm listening.*

"I canna marry," Winslow said slowly. "Not just ye, lass," he said, releasing his hold on her and abruptly stalking away.

"No one refuses a direct order from the king," Augustin said in clipped tones.

Lady Eyreka's gasp echoed her own. It would seem more than her own father's wishes were to be considered. The enormity of her situation hit home with the force of a cudgel. She swayed on her feet, but caught herself, shrugging off the offered assistance. Winslow would forfeit his life if he disobeyed the king!

Winslow stopped halfway across the hall. His arms dropped back to his sides; his massive hands clenched into formidable looking fists. "I dinna mean to hurt ye, lass," he rasped, then turned back toward the doorway and disappeared from sight.

"Never you," Genvieve whispered, and for the second time, no one appeared to hear her. "'Tis not your hand that wielded the dagger of mistrust, nor you who plunged it into my breast."

She finally turned her gaze away from the door and noticed that her cousin and his wife were watching her intently. For the first time, Genvieve was not sorry she had no voice.

⁂

GENVIEVE SAT ALONE in her chamber, sorrow lancing sharply through her breast. *Francois, why did you leave me?* No voice answered her silent cry. No words of comfort reached her straining ears. I do not even have a raven-haired babe to cuddle and care for, she thought bitterly. Even that gift was cruelly torn from me.

The pain of her miscarriages returned with a vengeance, as fresh as it had been nearly a dozen years before. She tried to close her eyes against the pain, but she saw herself double over as if in pain. She saw her gown soaked with blood, Francois's babe's lifeblood.

With a groan of agony, she pushed herself up on the bed, and dropped her head in her hands, and asked God, why did she have to give up the man she adored? Why had she been unable to carry either of their babes to term?

Genvieve swept the tangled strands of hair out of her eyes and swung her legs over the edge of the bed, letting them dangle for a brief moment before pushing off the bed.

She began to pace the small chamber while scenes of her past flashed before her. It was as if her tortured mind was forcing her to relive the past. By the tenth trip past the arrowslit, the air had grown thick, and her breathing had become labored. She drew in a breath but could not get enough air. Desperate for a breath of fresh air, moments away from hysteria, she bolted for the door.

With no memory of opening her chamber door or descending the steps, she jolted out of her panic as a fresh, cool breeze hit her in the face. She gasped, drawing in more air than she needed. After a few deep breaths, her breathing slowed and returned to normal.

The full moon lit her way, as she walked around the back of the holding to the walled herb garden. The subtle scent of rosemary wafted up to greet her as the hem of her sleeping gown brushed against the fragrant herb.

The cinder path wound through the groupings of plantings, leading her to the far wall and the little used side door. Thoughts of escape filled her with each step she took.

Freedom.

Blinding need to be free of Merewood's walls twisted through her, nearly robbing her of the precious breath she had just recovered. Her heartbeat picked up speed and she could feel her life's blood beginning to pound through her veins. Her steps gathered momentum until she was running toward the wooden door.

She grasped the handle and tugged, not even thinking to muffle the sound of the hinges. They creaked and groaned, but the door opened. She slipped through, not bothering to stop and close it. Unsure of where the path would lead, she slowed her pace to a fast walk.

Soon her thoughts were tangled up with the past. A rustling in the underbrush startled her. When she turned toward the sound, she saw Francois's beloved face. Her silent scream erupted from the pit of her stomach. She began to run again and with each pounding footstep, visions of their raven-haired babes haunted her. The crack of a twig made her jump and look behind her. The specter of her betrothed, Guy, seemed to float toward her.

She stifled another scream of terror and ran on. Her head pounded viciously, marking time with each footfall. Pain enveloped her, wrapping her frayed feelings about her until she thought to suffocate. A sudden splashing sound echoed in the stillness of the night, but she ignored it, driven on by the pain in her heart and heaviness in her soul.

The sudden chill of the lake water broke through the demons of her past. Icy fingers of dread curled at the base of her spine and crept slowly upward toward her pounding heart. Breast-deep in weed-choked water, she tried, but could not move. Her struggles bound her tighter, until she was held fast by unseen ropes of green, tangled beyond her ability to free herself.

Genvieve tried to cry out for help, but only the broken sound of her useless voice echoed in the vast emptiness.

A sudden sinking sensation caught her by surprise. She tried to ignore it, but then distinctly felt it again. The soft lake bottom was slowly pulling her under.

There was no one to help her.

By morning, she would be dead.

Chapter Ten

Genvieve floated toward the bright white light, a sense of peace surrounding her, easing the stabbing pain in her lungs and brutal pounding in her head. She heard a familiar voice calling to her—*Francois!* As she opened her mouth to call out to him, she felt herself being flung on her stomach and pummeled on her back. Strange words rained over her head. The bright white light faded along with her husband's words, *'Tis not yet time.*

⇒⇒⇒⇐⇐⇐

"Damn yer eyes!" MacInness cursed. "Breathe."

MacInness straddled Genvieve, pressing down again and trying to force the rest of the lake water up and out of her.

"Dinna think to take the coward's way out, lass. I wilna let ye."

Her body jerked beneath him. "That's it," he coaxed, moving off of her. While her body rid itself of seemingly gallons of lake water, he held her. When the convulsions began to slow down, he pulled her closer, hoping that all that was left were the spasms of a body that had borne far more than it should have to.

Holding her wet body against his, he felt the spasms beginning to lessen. His body trembled when she finally settled down.

Breathing deeply, he wished he knew what to do with her. God help him, he didn't want to marry. Couldn't in good conscience marry when his heart still yearned for another.

"What am I goin' to do with ye, lass?"

He brushed tangled damp strands of ebony hair off her face. She shifted and he moaned when she nuzzled against his palm. He thought of the promised holding and taking Genvieve to wife and knew it would be a mistake. His heart belonged to another.

He drew her close and felt the strong echo of her heart pounding in rhythm with his own. He cared for the lass and recognized the depth of that caring when he saw her struggling to free herself from the weed-choked water off the west shore of the lake. But he didn't love her.

He slowly stood, the precious burden in his arms achingly familiar. "Hang on, lass," he rasped. "'Tis just through the wood."

This time his grip did not slacken. Though exhausted from the eerie battle fought beneath the surface of the lake against deadly weeds, and then expelling the lake water from her body, he was more than ready to walk back through the woods across the clearing to the keep.

One thought after another plagued him as his steady stride brought them closer to the small postern gate. Had she left it open so that he would follow her? Had she meant to get so tangled up in the lake bottom and weeds? Would she rather face death itself than pledge her life to him or was it his refusal to marry her?

"MacInness!" The familiar sound of Patrick's voice stopped him short. Before he had taken three steps, his vassal was at his side.

The man who had willingly pledged his sword arm nearly a dozen years ago laid a hand on his arm. MacInness met Patrick's searching gaze, shook his head slightly, knowing his friend would understand his need for silence. Too many emotions tangled up inside him all at once.

Patrick reached across the space between them and touched a

hand to her neck. After a moment, he looked at MacInness. "She's alive, then."

MacInness nodded and kept walking. He had to get her back to her bedchamber and in front of a fire. The risk of lung fever was great.

"Was she alone?"

Patrick's question was the first one MacInness had asked himself when he first saw Genvieve struggling to save herself. He nodded.

"She didn't try to drown herself," Patrick's voice sounded flat, emotionless.

It was how MacInness had felt the moment he heard the faint cry and rushed to the lake in time to see her go under. His warrior's training took over and he acted without need for thought. Once she was safe on shore, he began the arduous task of expelling the water from her body. The sound of her stomach rebelling had been sweet.

"I dinna think she meant to."

Patrick shared the same strong religious beliefs. Neither of them wanted to believe she'd given in to despair and tried to kill herself.

By the time they'd reached the postern gate, MacInness had come to a decision. He'd wed the lass to save her from herself.

⇶⇷

GENVIEVE WOKE WITH a jolt, dragging air into her lungs. The coughing fit had her stomach clenching in agony.

"Easy, lass. Dinna try to move too fast."

She opened her eyes and her heart actually hurt. The man she'd been told to marry, the one who didn't want her, was sitting beside the bed. His dark expression belied the gentle tone he'd used.

"How did I get here?" Her voice cracked and sounded like

nails scraping over a slick surface, but she needed him to know the rest. "I don't remember how I got to the lake."

He was silent for so long, she was afraid he would not answer her. Finally, he did, "I thought ye were made of sterner stuff, lass."

She opened her mouth to speak, but he glared at her.

"That ye'd try to take yer own life, just because I refused to marry ye—"

She bolted up and grabbed for his hand, shaking her head, willing him to understand that was not how it happened.

He started to tug his hand free, then must have thought better of it. "I dinna want to marry, lass. 'Tisn't yer fault."

Genvieve felt tears welling in her eyes. She blinked furiously; she didn't want to appear weak, even though she knew in her heart the Scotsman thought she'd tried to kill herself. God, please let her voice work. Winslow squeezed her hand and stood and walked to the door.

"No!" This time the cry came from the pit of her stomach and sounded like a scalded cat. But he stopped and turned around.

He waited, but she didn't know what else to say, didn't trust that her voice wouldn't bring the servants running to see who was torturing small animals in her chamber.

"I'll be back, lass," he said. "Rest now."

Genvieve slumped against the pillow when he shut the door. The urge to weep swept over her. Alone, she finally gave in.

⇶⇷

MACINNESS HEARD HER sobs and paused, clenching his hands into fists, waiting for the urge to go back and hold Genvieve to pass. The stark need shook his resolve not to care any deeper than he did. He'd given his heart already; he had no room in it for another.

As he made his way across the hall, he roused a servant and

had her go find Lady Eyreka. It was the least he could do, sending someone to watch over Genvieve.

Before he made it to the door, he heard Garrick call him. He didn't want to talk to anyone right now, especially his overlord.

"What happened?" Garrick demanded catching up to him.

"The lass had a little trouble by the lake."

Garrick never showed any emotion when he asked, "She tried to—"

"Nay," MacInness bit out before Garrick could finish the question. If he denied it enough times, then perhaps the niggling doubt in the back of his skull would be satisfied.

"We need to talk." The set of the other man's jaw didn't bode well.

MacInness inclined his head and motioned for Garrick to follow him outside. He breathed deeply of the cool night air and headed toward the stable. Before he was halfway there, Garrick grabbed his arm.

"That's far enough."

MacInness looked around them to make sure no one had followed them from the hall. Though most of the servants had been sleeping, it was best to be certain. He didn't trust that whoever had attacked Genvieve would eventually find their way to Merewood Keep.

"There's no one else here," Garrick began. "What's the real reason you cannot marry Genvieve?"

MacInness's breath whooshed out and his gut clenched. "I—"

"Is there someone else?" Garrick prodded when MacInness fell silent.

"Ye might say that." He did not want to be having this conversation at all, let alone with his overlord.

"I was there."

A feeling of dread washed over MacInness. "Where were ye, mon?"

The other man crossed his arms in front of his chest and stared.

MacInness's Scots granny had *the sight* and at odd times, he felt shimmerings of awareness. He braced himself.

"That day in the herb garden," Garrick said. "If I hadn't been so shocked by Jillian's professing her love for me, I would have gutted you without blinking an eye."

MacInness nodded. "I'd have done the same, then skinned ye."

Garrick didn't flinch. "You kept her safe," he said. "Brought her out of that hellish situation."

MacInness remembered it well; it was the first time he had become aware of his feelings for the lady.

Garrick's stance became rigid. "The day she rode out and you followed…"

"I told the lass to turn back," MacInness began.

Garrick looked away and then back. The pain in his overlord's gaze told MacInness what he'd known. "I don't know what I'd have done if she'd died or lost the babe."

MacInness swallowed against the lump in his throat. "I owe her my life."

The man he now counted as a friend reached out and placed a hand on MacInness's shoulder. "Jillian loves me."

A shaft of pain slicing through his already aching gut. "Aye."

"You need to let go."

The need to pound someone senseless nearly overwhelmed his iron-clad control. "I canna."

"She's my wife—"

"And I've pledged my life to protect her."

"But you have feelings—"

MacInness raked a hand through his hair. "Can ye not let it go at that, mon?"

Garrick's arms slid to his sides, and he fisted his hands. "She's—"

"A wonderful woman, courageous, gentle, beautiful."

"And she belongs—"

"To ye." MacInness nodded. "And I'd give my life for her and would never go back on my word to never give her a reason not to trust me." He wished he hadn't made that vow, but the look in her eyes had swayed him. "'Tis why I canna marry."

Garrick got right into his face and ground out, "No, 'tis why you must."

MacInness felt the other man's anger then and knew it was time to let go of the hope that someday Lady Jillian would change her mind and leave her husband. "Genvieve won't have me."

His overlord stepped back, relaxed his stance and rubbed the side of his head. "She will."

MacInness wondered if Patrick had told Garrick just what took place earlier. He disregarded the thought. His own vassal had given his word not to speak of it and no one would hear how Genvieve came to be in the lake or why he thought she'd gone there. "I've got to go," he started walking.

"Wait."

He paused.

"Genvieve needs you."

"She doesna."

"What if the bastards that attacked her come looking for her?" Garrick said. "Will you be content knowing she won't likely live through another attack? That you could have protected her?"

The truth of the other man's words hit him like a blow to his midsection. His breath rasped out as he wondered why God, in His infinite wisdom, saddled MacInness with a woman who couldn't speak but had still managed to make it plain that she didn't want to marry him.

He was a propertied man, battle-hardened, but not afraid of hard work. He might not be titled, but he'd have Sedgeworth Keep now, even though he didn't want it. He'd be able to help feed his clan...

Fighting against it wouldn't change the inevitable. His shoulders fell in resignation.

"I'll speak to de Chauret in the mornin'."

CHAPTER ELEVEN

A FORTNIGHT LATER, Genvieve could not believe she'd married. Though barely able to speak her vows, she and the man who'd rescued her not once but twice lay beside her unmoving. She knew he wasn't asleep.

The devil in her had her reaching out and poking him in the ribs. He shuddered, and Genvieve's hopes crushed in on her. The passionate kisses they'd shared were just that and would never lead to more. Her husband hadn't lied about not wanting to marry; he just hadn't told her his reasons.

MacInness's loud sigh didn't help the way she was feeling. *Merde*, she didn't want to be facing another husband she barely knew across the marriage bed. She'd worked herself up to accepting another Norman as husband, but he'd died in battle, and Father had promised she'd never have to marry again. He'd lied.

Rolling over and away, as close to the edge of the bed as possible, Genvieve called herself a fool. Only a fool would continue to hold out hope when in her heart she knew the truth—she'd already had her chance at love and lost him to a Saxon's blade. This time, her marriage would be payment to the man who'd save her life…twice.

The bed creaked and she went absolutely still. When her cousin had told her MacInness changed his mind and they would wed, she suspected it had to do with that night at the lake. Her husband was a born protector of innocents…and she'd not been innocent in years. Still, she couldn't help the way her body tensed and stiffened as he shifted closer. His heat radiated through the thin cotton sleeping gown she'd slipped into when waiting for him to come to their chamber.

"I wilna have ye thinkin' I'm no' a mon of my word, lass."

Genvieve turned to her husband, ready for rejection, and was swept into his arms.

"I didna want to marry, lass, but I never said I didna want to bed ye."

He slid one hand down to her backside and pressed his lower body against hers. Years of tamping down her physical needs melted away as he boldly pressed his hardness against her, letting her feel his desire. Her womb clenched, and she felt her inner muscles tighten in anticipation.

Winslow. Her lips moved, though she'd trained herself not to make any sound when she spoke because of the snide comments about the sound of it when her back was turned.

He bent his head to press his lips to her throat.

There. Ah yes, right there.

She wanted him—now! Her arms tightened around him, and she arched her body up off the bed. His amber eyes darkened, and he pinned her to the bed with his hips. His lips and tongue blazed a heated path along the length of her collarbone. Her woman's core clenched again, and she felt the familiar liquid warmth filling her.

The need to have him overwhelmed her. She lifted her hips, urging him to press down harder. He went absolutely still. Had she misjudged the man? Did he think her overbold?

"Lass." Her gaze locked with his. "I dinna want to hurt ye."

Tears filled her eyes and she let them fall. *You won't.*

He waited a heartbeat, then bent his head and took her breast in his mouth.

Someone moaned. She didn't care who. Her husband had

latched on to her as if he were starving. His wicked tongue flicked and teased her taut nipple through the thin cotton. When his hand cupped the weight of her other breast, she shifted her legs wider in invitation.

Winslow…

He lifted his head, his eyes black with passion. Before she would ask him, he slid his free hand down to inch up her gown and draw it up over her head.

She gasped at the heat of him pressing against her. Her body went limp in response. His groan surprised her.

"Ye're makin' it hard to wait."

Genvieve laughed.

He switched to her other breast, and her laughter died. He shifted off her and slid his hand along the curve of her waist and over her belly, dipping lower. A sharp, keening cry escaped from her lips as his fingers found her. Coaxed her. Stretched her.

His lips abandoned her breast, and he slipped his fingers from her, drawing his index finger into his mouth, sucking her essence from it.

"Honey," he rasped. "Ye taste of it."

"Winslow!" The ragged cry sounded like a cat being skinned, but she didn't care. She wanted him inside her, would die if he didn't take her right now!

She tugged on him to pull him back on top of her, but he shook his head.

"I've no' finished." His words shot straight to her core as he sucked his middle finger into his mouth.

Her heart stumbled in her breast.

"Now, where were we?"

She shook her head; speech was beyond her.

He gripped her hips, lowered his head, and kissed her belly.

She shivered.

He looked up and grinned. "I've a need to taste ye, lass."

Her breath snagged, and for a moment, she couldn't breathe. *Taste her?* She'd heard decadent rumors of such, but never—

Taking her hesitation as permission, he lifted her to his mouth and plundered.

Each swirl of his tongue unleased a cry from the depths of her being. Her hands fisted around the bed linens as he devoured her. Alternating licks with the thrust of his talented tongue, her husband urged her higher.

Her body ached for more, sought the bliss of release.

But he left her there on the brink, lowered her to the bed, and growled, "Ye're food enough for a starvin' mon."

His words had no meaning; she was beyond thought, craving completion only he could give her.

Her voice sounded gravelly to her ears, but she ignored it, telling him, "I need—"

Grabbing her hips, he thrust into her and filled her to the hilt.

Her hips lifted to meet each hungry thrust. His moans of pleasure urged her to take more, to give more. Her hands slid down to grab his muscled backside and press him impossibly closer. He growled and thrust home.

Her world exploded as her release ripped through her.

His shout of triumph roared in her ears as he went absolutely still.

Genvieve felt the incredible warmth of his seed filling her. Tears welled in her eyes at the realization that there would be no babe…ever.

Instead of pulling out of her, Winslow slid his hand beneath her, splaying it across her backside. In a smooth move, he rolled them over until she lay on top of him. "Ye've killed me, lass."

The wicked grin on his face belied the fact that she hadn't. She couldn't hold back her smile.

He kissed her full on the mouth, and she tasted herself on his lips. *Forbidden.*

He chuckled when she stiffened. "What's done between a mon and his wife isna wrong, lass."

When she didn't answer him, he nipped her shoulder. "If ye give me a moment to catch my breath, I've no' yet satisfied my appetite, lass."

⇢⇠

MacInness pulled his wife against his heart. She'd surprised him with her passionate response to his loving. But when he'd tasted her, God in heaven, he thought he'd burst and spill his seed on the bed linens.

He'd dug deep for control, though his wife's body threatened to destroy it. Her lush curves, and the way she trusted him to sup from her bounty, even when he realized she'd never experienced it before, went straight to his battered heart.

Satisfaction at being the first to pleasure her with his lips and tongue filled him. *Bloody Sassenach husband of hers didn't know how to properly bed a woman.* A Highlander instinctively knew how to pleasure a woman…and take her to the stars…more than once. There was no pleasure if ye had a frigid, weeping, wailing woman beneath ye. 'Twas a mon's job to make his woman hot for him, and he would reap the rewards.

She sighed and cuddled closer. MacInness swept his hand up into her silken hair and held her head to his pounding heart, wanting…nay, needing her to see she wasn't the only one affected by their lovemaking.

Contentment filled him until he felt something wet sliding down his side. Tears? *Had he hurt her?* He pulled out of her, hoping his fear was unfounded.

"I didna think I hurt ye." He leaned back far enough so that he could see her face. She shook her head. "Well, what is it then?" He tried to gentle his tone, but from the way her eyes widened, he hadn't.

"Genvieve, I'm yer husband now," he said gentling his hold on her, stroking the tip of his finger across one eyebrow and then the other. "There isna anythin' ye canna tell me."

She shook her head at him, more tears slipping from beneath

her thick, dark lashes.

He sighed, brushed a kiss to her brow and laid her on the bed. Her eyes shot open.

"Dinna worry, lass, I've not lost me desire to have another taste."

He slipped from the bed, walked over to the small table by the wall and grabbed the linen square next to the pitcher of water. Handing it to her, he commanded, "Blow yer nose and dry yer eyes, and then tell me what ails ye, lass, so I can fix it."

The dam broke loose. His wife must have been holding back a year's worth of tears.

"*Bollocks*," he cursed beneath his breath. When she took a swing at him, he knew she'd heard him. With a sigh of resignation, he got back into bed and pulled her into his arms.

Cradling her against his heart, he wondered what he'd do with her. His plans never included a wife. Holding her as she cried, he wondered how much longer she'd be at it. He did not want to give her reason for more tears. The lass had to run dry soon, didn't she? "Are ye done yet?"

His wife blew her nose and tried to hand the saturated linen back to him. He looked at it and shook his head. "Keep it."

Finally, she dragged in a breath and settled down.

She was silent for so long, he wondered if she'd tell him or make him wait and then an unwelcome thought filled him. "Dinna tell me ye've left a lover behind."

Her snort of derision surprised him, and had him promising, "He wilna live for long. Tell me the mon's name and I'll take care of him for ye."

Genvieve tightened her hold on him, making him wonder if she did have a lover. "Lass?"

"I can't have children," she rasped.

MacInness didn't answer right away, unsure of what she expected of him. When she trembled in his arms, he knew she was afraid he'd be angry with her.

"Dinna fear, lassie, I've probably a bairn or two. I dinna need any more."

She shoved out of his arms. "Probably?" she asked, wincing at the sound of her own voice. "Don't you know?"

He cupped her cheek in one hand and brushed his thumb near the corner of her mouth. "I'm a careful mon, lass. I dinna have bairns, though I've a nephew and six nieces."

Her gaze latched onto his and for a moment he saw raw need flare in hers. *She wants children.* "How do ye know ye canna have bairns?" He shouldn't push her to speak when he knew it pained her, but he had to know.

She closed her eyes and told him about her first husband. His stomach roiled at the thought of his wife losing babes. It was a miracle she hadn't bled to death.

He slid his hand around to the back of her head and gently pushed it to his shoulder. "Ye should've told me. I wouldna want to risk ye having bairns at such cost to ye, lass."

She shrugged. "It won't matter, I've never quickened again." Her anguished gaze held his. "After I lost the second babe, the healer declared me barren." The words she uttered actually hurt more than the ache in her throat.

MacInness rubbed a hand up and down her spine. The delicacy of her frame wasn't what he expected. Her curves were lushly ripe. He'd have thought her bones would be sturdier.

"Dinna fash yerself, lass. I'll no' get ye with child," he promised, pressing his lips to the top of her head. "Yer my wife now," he rasped. "And I protect what's mine."

He waited for her answer, tensed for it. When he heard the soft sound of rhythmic breathing, he knew he'd eased her mind, and she'd fallen asleep. His lie lay heavy upon him, but he'd slit his own throat before he'd tell his wife the truth.

He wanted bairns.

CHAPTER TWELVE

SHE SENSED SHE was alone before she opened her eyes. When she touched the empty place beside her, it felt cool to the touch; Winslow had left their bed some time ago. Unsure of what her reception would be now that she was married in the eyes of God, she put off the inevitable going down to the hall.

Closing her eyes brought the memory of last night's lovemaking rushing back. The lethal combination of deft touches and mind-numbing kisses had her breath quickening. Her husband was truly gifted in bed.

But she was no giddy bride that could afford to lie around in bed, savoring every touch, every taste. There was work to be done, and though she may not be looking forward to the task, servants to greet, and duties to see to.

The water in the pitcher was tepid but would do. She'd ask for a hot bath later. For now, she washed away the evidence of last night, sorry that the musky scent was gone, replaced by the familiar scent of lavender.

Someone had laid out a clean chainse and bliaut of the palest gray. Not ready to summon help, and more than ready to begin her day, Genvieve dressed, taking the time to brush her hair until it shone. First impressions were important, and she wanted Sedgeworth's people to like her.

The finishing touch would be the corded belt she'd worn

yesterday. Her hand flew to her throat. If only she hadn't lost her grandfather's cross. The knight her mother had sent to bring her back to London had carried it to her as proof that her mother was gravely ill. Shaking the bleak thoughts free, she walked to the door.

It opened and her husband's powerful form filled the doorframe. His gaze raked her from head to toe and back. When his amber eyes turned molten with desire, her belly clenched, and her breasts felt heavy. She wanted him to make love to her...nay, needed him to.

He didn't move while she let her gaze travel over his broad shoulders, taking in the cream-colored linen shirt and red-and-gray plaid kilt. Her husband was warrior-strong, but his hands had gentled last night. But what was one night's loving, when compared to the next twenty years of day-to-day living? She needed to get to know her husband, understand the way he thought and hopefully come to an understanding between them.

Mayhap she could make up for her lack of ability to give him babes if she smoothed the way between Sedgeworth's people and their new overlord. After last night, she had no doubt at all they would do well in the marriage bed.

She smiled.

The front of his kilt moved, and he closed his eyes. "Ye'd best stop yer lookin', lass," he said. He opened his eyes and pinned her with his gaze. "Else I'll no' finish trainin' with the guards. I've no time for dallyin'."

Her smile grew wider. Genvieve hadn't affected Francois like that. Had she? She shook her head knowing she hadn't.

Winslow groaned out loud, strode across the room and gathered her in his arms. His heart pounded, but the rhythm matched hers. He bent his head and captured her lips, urging her to let him taste her with the tip of his tongue.

She moaned and his tongue thrust inside, mimicking the lovemaking that had made her daft last night. Her bones literally melted. She lost her balance, but he crushed her against him. He grew harder as he held her in place with his big hands.

Blind and deaf to everything but the passion between them, neither one heard the discrete cough, or noticed the servant standing in the doorway until she coughed. Winslow lifted his head and cleared his throat. "It seems we've been missed, wife."

Genvieve jolted, as heat suffused her cheeks. She pinched his side to get his attention, his hands were still cupping her bottom.

He grinned at her, and called out, "We'll be down directly."

She let her forehead rest against his chest. It wouldn't matter that one of the servants had seen them together, mayhap talk would begin that the new overlord was a man who cared for his wife.

Cared for. Did he?

She knew he enjoyed bedding her, but being with her when she couldn't hold even the simplest conversations? He'd grow tired of her grating voice, and if it didn't heal, her silent presence. She couldn't stand the sound of her own voice, and if it didn't return to normal, would probably stop speaking altogether.

With a sigh of regret, knowing she had no control over her life until she could speak again bothered her, but it was time to meet the servants and begin the day's list of tasks.

Descending the steps into the hall, Genvieve was pleased to see the remnants of yesterday's wedding feast had been cleared away and sweet-smelling rushes had been spread across the floor. The scent of freshly baked bread wafted toward her as one of the serving women carried a plate toward the long table against the side wall.

Winslow led her into the hall and over to the table laden with their morning meal. He nodded to a young woman with pale-blonde hair. The woman curtseyed, then walked over to Genvieve. With hand motions, the woman gestured with her hand to her stomach and then pretending she held a cup, mimicked drinking.

Genvieve's eyes welled with tears that spilled over. She reached for her husband's hand, her anchor since the day she'd woken without the ability to speak. Bringing his hand to her lips she kissed it, then pressed her cheek against the freckles sprinkled across his knuckles. He'd taught one of the women to communicate with her.

"Beatrice is here to serve us, lass."

She nodded to the woman, dried her eyes with her free hand, and let her husband lead her to the table.

A few of the household knights introduced themselves to her, all seemed to know MacInness. She wondered why, but didn't have the means to ask. One or two of them didn't hide their dislike of her husband. Their reaction worried her. She'd ask Winslow later, when they were alone and he could watch her lips while she asked, he'd become adept at reading them.

As the servants were clearing the table a gray-haired woman hurried over to the table. She curtseyed, then rose. "Welcome to Sedgeworth Keep, milady," she said, spreading her hands wide encompassing the hall with the gesture.

Genvieve looked at her husband. He nodded, as if he knew she wouldn't be able to speak if she could. "Anna runs the kitchens and will help ye with the food stores, lass." He reached over and took her hand in his. "If ye need me, just fist yer hand and put it to yer heart, like this."

Emotions she thought long dead surfaced. That he would go to such lengths to ease her way as mistress in their new home, where no one knew her but all would have to answer to her, filled in the empty void that her first husband's death had left behind. And that's when she stopped denying what her heart already knew—she loved Winslow.

She blinked away the tears, leaned over, and pressed her lips to his. Winslow's lips were cool to the touch but warmed quickly, softening as he kissed her back. He'd not bargained for a wife, but he'd gained one the moment he made the decision to intervene and rescue her, from what she now knew would have been her death.

"There's a lass," he said, brushing a hand to her cheek, sweeping a tear away. After they'd eaten, he helped her to her feet and walked with her and Anna to the kitchens. With a kiss to her forehead, he left.

The morning wasn't as difficult as she'd thought. With a few gestures and mouthed words, she and Anna had developed a rhythm, counting the barrels of flour, grain, and salted meats. Thirteen in all. The last of the barrels was recorded, and she was due in the hall to oversee the midday meal.

Brushing the strand of hair from her eyes, she silently asked, *How many will be there?*

Anna watched closely and finally nodded, smiling. "Most of the household knights spend the day either training, patrolling, or collecting revenues from the crofters. There will be a handful."

She'd have to ask her husband how often the revenues were collected. It wouldn't do to take too much from their people.

Anna was right; there were only a handful, but that handful did not linger over the meal. Her husband didn't appear, and she'd heard he wouldn't be stopping until the evening meal because he and his men were training in the lower bailey.

Why did they need to train if there was no war going on? No one was nearby to answer her question. She hurried through the passageway and was nearly run over by a tall black-haired knight. She stepped out of the way at the last moment, but he still knocked into her, scowling at her the entire time. He saw her, why didn't he slow down, or move out of the way, as she tried to do?

Two hours later, exhausted from helping to organize one of the storerooms below the hall, Genvieve had all but forgotten the mishap.

"Do I have time for a bath?" she slowly mouthed to Anna.

She had to slow down and exaggerate the words, but the second time she asked, Anna nodded. "Aye, milady. I'll have hot water brought up directly."

"Thank you."

Trudging up the steps, she wondered if tomorrow would

have as many tasks waiting for her. Although more tired than she'd ever admit, she'd enjoyed herself today. She felt needed, and she hadn't felt that way in a long time.

By the time she'd reached her chamber, Beatrice was knocking on the doorframe. She smiled at the younger woman delighted that the servants had arrived with the first of the buckets for her bath. *"Wonderful!"*

The other woman must have been watching closely as Genvieve didn't have to repeat herself. Relieved, she sat down and waited while the servants filled the wooden tub. They left as soon as the last drop was poured.

Beatrice handed her a small-lidded jar.

Genvieve opened it and the scent of wildflowers wafted up. She breathed deeply and looked over at the servant. She smiled and Beatrice returned the smile.

"I'll just put a dash into the water for you before I help you undress."

Suddenly sleepy, Genvieve let herself be pampered. Sinking into the scented water, she felt her body begin to relax. She hadn't realized she was so tense. Beatrice talked while she helped to wash Genvieve's hair.

"Such color, milady," Beatrice rasped. "I've always wanted dark hair…with not a smidgeon of red in it."

Genvieve shrugged as she mouthed the words, *"My mother's hair is the most glorious shade of chestnut."* She sighed. *"I've always wanted dark-brown hair. Black is just so plain."*

Beatrice frowned, and waited for Genvieve to repeat herself.

When she did, the servant snorted, trying not to laugh. "Isn't that just the way? We all want what we don't have."

By the time the bath water had cooled off, Genvieve was dressed in a fresh chainse and dark-green bliaut. She'd not seen her husband all day and wondered if all went well during training.

"Milady!" Anna sounded frantic. "Come quick, his lordship—"

Not waiting for Beatrice to hand her the belted girdle, she dashed out of the room, ran for the stairs.

Anna stood at the bottom, wringing her hands and Genvieve noticed splotches of blood across the hem of the woman's chainse.

"Where is he?" she demanded, her voice grating harshly, as she spoke aloud. "How badly is he hurt?" Judging from the look on Anna's face, it was not good.

Following the older woman into the hall, she skidded to a stop halfway across the room. Her husband's body lay on the tabletop. Before she could ask why they hadn't brought him upstairs, she noticed a familiar face among the handful of men standing around the table. The knight who'd rudely knocked into her earlier. As if he felt her gaze on him, he looked up and glared at her.

Hand to her throat, she wondered why he would have such a distaste for her. She didn't know the man and would swear she'd never seen him before today. Her husband moaned and she hurried to his side. Brushing her hand across his sweaty brow, she looked at Anna and mouthed the words, *"What's wrong with him?"*

The older woman shook her head, and answered, "I'm not sure, four men carried him inside and I immediately went to fetch you."

"I need—"

"Hot water and dry cloths," Anna said without waiting for her to finish. "I've sent Beatrice and she should be—"

Genvieve ignored the rest of what the woman was saying, concentrating on the slow rise and fall of her husband's chest. Letting her eyes and her hands guide her, she checked for obvious signs of injury. She motioned for one of the men to help her lift him.

A young knight stepped forward and braced himself against Winslow's bulk and lifted her husband, moving around to hold him from the front; Genvieve was able to slip behind him. A trickle of blood on his neck had her stomach roiling and her fingers deftly searching the back of his head for a cut hidden by his shaggy red hair.

She felt the warmth of his blood before she realized she'd found the gash and drew back her hand. The sight of Winslow's blood on her fingers had spots forming before her eyes. Her head felt oddly disconnected from her body.

"Milady." Anna braced an arm around Genvieve's back. The contact grounded her so she could do what she had to.

"We'll clean it out first," Genvieve's voice grated over the words.

The older woman nodded. "Then see if it'll need threads."

Genvieve suddenly realized the men were still in the room. She motioned for them to leave. All but two did her bidding—one was the dark-haired knight, and the other, the warrior who helped her lift her husband.

"You're to blame for this," the dark one bit out.

Appalled, she stepped back needing the distance between them. The young knight who'd helped her lift Winslow strode back into the hall. "You don't know that for certain, Giles," the younger man defended her. "Let it go."

While Genvieve watched, the younger man grabbed a hold of the dark knight and dragged him from the room.

Working together, she cleansed the wound while Anna held Winslow, saying, "He's trouble, that one."

Genvieve paused in her ministrations to ask, *"Why?"*

Anna read her lips and shrugged. "He was loyal to Owen, the last lord of Sedgeworth Keep."

Loyalty was sometimes misplaced. Genvieve hoped the man wouldn't continue to cause trouble.

It wasn't until after Winslow had been carried to their chamber and put to bed that she learned what happened. Another of her husband's household knights spoke up.

"No one was with MacInness when he walked to the smithy right before the midday meal."

"I was told he wasn't joining us."

The knight waited a moment then nodded letting her know

that he understood the words she mouthed. "MacInness said he wanted to check on the state of the keep's arms," he explained. "Not much has been done since Owen was summoned to London."

Genvieve listened while smoothing the linen over her husband's still form. Worry that he had not yet wakened gnawed at her. Was it something more than the blow to the head? Had she missed something important?

"The men grew restless when their overlord didn't return as promised," he continued. "So one of them went to find him."

"Thank you for your help, Simon," Anna said walking with him to the door. "Best have someone keep watch 'til the master wakens."

Genvieve's hand trembled as she brushed a strand of bright red off Winslow's forehead. He flinched. A good sign. Wasn't it?

"*I'll be all right,*" she told Anna, grateful the older woman could read lips. "*Serve the evening meal without me.*"

Anna nodded. "He'll be fine, milady."

Genvieve's gaze met hers. "*I know.*"

With the closing of the door, all of her worries surfaced because she no longer had to put on a brave show in front of MacInness's men. She sat on the edge of the bed and ran her fingers along Winslow's brow.

No one was there to comment on the wounded sound of her voice. In a broken rasp, she pleaded, "Please wake up."

He turned toward her touch. Had he heard her? Encouraged, she pressed her lips where her fingers had been. His skin was cool to the touch. "There is no fever. Why won't you wake up?"

She'd only just acknowledged the depth of her feelings for her husband but hadn't told him. Would he die before she had the chance? *No*, she vowed. He would not.

"I've a powerful need for you, husband," her voice cracked as she continued. "I've only just found you." Her voice sounded horrible to her ears, but Winslow couldn't hear her, and no one else was around. What difference did it make?

He shifted, and she hoped he was moving toward wakefulness. She'd never encountered an injury like this before.

"Winslow," she leaned close to his ear. "I love you," she whispered. "Don't leave me," she begged. Tears welled up and she let them fall. A drop hit him between the eyes, and he lifted his hand to brush it away.

She grabbed ahold of his hand, and squeezed it. "I'm right here, and I'll stay here until you waken," she promised. "Just don't die."

⸻

WINSLOW SLOWLY FOUGHT his way to the surface, battling against the blackness that held him down. The heavy weight on his chest worried him; something held him down...an enemy!

He tried to shift the weight off him, when he recognized the scent and feel of the woman. He opened his eyes and blinked to clear his vision. What he was seeing couldn't be real.

His wife had lit a candle by the bedside and lay across him, her arms holding tight to him in her sleep, as if she were afraid to let him go.

"Well now, lass," he rasped. "Dinna fash yerself on my account."

She jolted awake and knocked his chin with her elbow. "Winslow," she said, her voice grating. "You're awake...I've got to get Anna."

He reached out and held her, when she would have bolted from his side. "Stay, lass," he asked, "I've a powerful headache."

"*I was afraid,*" she mouthed.

"I dinna care how yer voice sounds, lass," he said. "I crave the sound of it, I didna think I'd hear it again."

She ignored how her voice would sound to ask, "What happened?"

"I was walking to the smithy, and someone clubbed me from

behind."

"Who?" She ignored the way her voice sounded.

"I dinna know," he paused. "But whoever it was didna stick around to see if they'd killed me."

"How do you know?" Lines of strain and worry were etched upon her brow. He raised his hand to smooth them.

"I'm still alive."

She nodded. "Winslow—"

He pulled her close. "Dinna start, lass. I'm here and that's enough for now."

He'd worry about who'd struck him later. Right now, he sorely needed the comforting touch of the woman in his arms.

CHAPTER THIRTEEN

MacInness was waiting when Patrick rode up the path to the postern gate of the holding. He stepped out of the shadows and raised his fist in the air. The other warrior reined in his horse and dismounted.

"Trouble?"

MacInness nodded and the ground moved beneath his feet. When his head stopped swimming Patrick was beside him and had an arm braced around him. "Someone tried to kill you?"

His head spun so he held still and answered, "Why would ye ask?"

Patrick grinned at him. "Well, you look like hell and cannot stand upright." When MacInness was steady, Patrick let go and grabbed the reins of his horse.

MacInness grunted, "I was on my way to the smithy and was hit from behind."

"Any idea who hit you?"

"I'm no' sure yet, but I dinna think it will be long before more trouble heads our way." MacInness rubbed the back of his neck. "Things have changed since Owen was overlord here."

Patrick clenched his jaw. "I'll speak to Garrick, then. He'll understand the need for me to leave Merewood's guard."

MacInness didn't want to admit that he'd feel better if he had his entire Irish Contingent surrounding him, but he couldn't take them back when they still served under Garrick of Merewood.

"Ye canna leave Merewood, ye pledged yer sword to Garrick when we finished serving Owen of Sedgeworth."

"And the king gave Merewood Keep to de Chauret."

A dark look crossed the Irishman's features, leaving MacInness to wonder what else the man knew. The man never spoke about his family or home without prying it from him with a flagon or two of mead.

"I dinna want to cause trouble with the new lord of Merewood."

They walked along the path back the way Patrick had come, away from the keep. "De Chauret is a good man."

"Ye trust the mon?"

Patrick nodded. "He nearly died trying to save his daughter."

MacInness hadn't heard the whole of that story yet. He'd been too preoccupied with the woman who'd become his wife.

"But he fought like a demon when he saw Lady Eyreka throw herself in front of his daughter," Patrick ground out. "He left his back unprotected … if William hadn't been there …"

"Canna be much of a fightin' mon, if he left his back unprotected."

Patrick paused by the bend in the road. "He loves Lady Eyreka."

MacInness wondered if the man had feelings for her and was glad to have it confirmed by a trusted source. "I'm sensin' trouble at Sedgeworth, mon."

His former vassal nodded. "Half of the guard was loyal to you and the other half…"

MacInness stared off in the distance. "To the bastard who let his wife beat Lady Jillian."

"But she's happy now, married to Garrick with a lusty-lunged babe."

They smiled. "Aye, young Alan's cries could wake the dead," MacInness agreed.

MacInness's gut knotted. He hadn't wanted to see her happy.

He'd hoped to return from the Highlands to find her miserable and regretting her decision not to take him up on his offer. But the fates conspired against him in favor of Garrick of Merewood. The lass loved her husband and her life.

"What about living with Norman rule?"

"Don't we all?"

MacInness grunted. "'Tis the truth, but I didna mean that and ye know it."

"Change comes," Patrick said before walking again. "Does your head pain you?"

"Only when me eyes are open," MacInness said, appreciating the gruff laughter of his friend. He'd missed it while he was away.

"Merewood Keep is well run. De Chauret is a fair man, who's open to change. Garrick's wife and mother are well protected." Patrick looked around him as if uneasy being so close to their former lord's holding. "I canna say the same for you and your lady wife."

"Genvieve," he stumbled over the name. "I still canna say it properly," he grunted. "When we both served Owen of Sedgeworth, before endin' our service to the mon, we were in the thick of things."

"The perspective is different when you're in the midst of the guard," Patrick added. "Yours is a lonely view, being at the top."

MacInness had thought the same. It was a large part of why he didn't want to accept the gift of Sedgeworth Keep. With it would come the running of the holding, caring for its people, and now it seemed a wife as well. A bonny lass. His mind wandered to the night they'd wed. The woman was passionate. A woman after his own heart who'd reveled in their lovemaking as much as he had.

"Does she know who attacked you?"

"I've yet to ask."

Patrick turned around and glared at him. "What do you know of her, or her people?" he asked. "How do you know she's doesn't subscribe to the Norman way of thinking that all Saxons and

Scots should be wiped out?"

MacInness had his friend by the throat before his brain registered that the man was gasping for breath. Horrified, he loosened his hold and stepped back. "I—"

Patrick rubbed at his throat, his face still red, but now with anger. "Be sure of the answer before you strike out at those of us who are your friends." He mounted his horse and set off at a cantor.

"Wait!" MacInness called out.

The warrior pulled back on the reins, but didn't turn around.

"I've feelin's for the lass."

Patrick looked over his shoulder. "Lady Jillian or your wife?"

MacInness rubbed his hand over his face. It was hard to admit, and the feelings had snuck up on him, but it was best to tell someone he trusted. But the words wouldn't come out.

Patrick turned his horse around. When he pulled to a stop, MacInness rasped, "My wife, Lady Genvieve."

Patrick stared at him. "So you no longer love Lady Jillian?"

MacInness's head shot up. "You knew?"

His friend nodded. "A few of us did, but we know you value honor above all else."

MacInness didn't know how he felt about others knowing of his love for Lady Jillian.

"'Tis why we followed you from Sedgeworth to Merewood," Patrick continued. "We hold honor and duty above all else."

Why hadn't his friend spoken to him about it? There'd been time enough. "But ye didna say anythin'."

"It wasn't important and at the time we were more concerned with making sure she was safe and that our new overlord didn't kill you."

The light of laughter in the other man's eyes eased the tension building inside of MacInness. "Well, there was a time or two when I'd gladly have beaten him bloody meself."

"About Lady Genvieve..." Patrick began.

"I care about the lass."

The other warrior nodded. "A good start, my friend." He picked up the reins again. "I'll speak to Garrick about releasing my men from his service, since he's no longer lord, but seneschal, our terms of service should have ended."

MacInness wasn't certain about that. "If he'll release ye, I'd be grateful if ye'd pledge yer sword to me."

Patrick grinned, "I've never gone back on my pledge to ye, ye damned Scot."

"But yer—"

"Pledged to Garrick of Merewood because we followed you. My sword is yours first."

MacInness felt his throat tighten. He'd always hoped his men's loyalty hadn't shifted when they'd followed him from Sedgeworth to Merewood Keep. Confirmation of that hope set his mind at ease. "All right then, mon," he said. "See if Kelly and Eamon can join ye."

"I've heard from Sean."

MacInness smiled. "Did he follow young Roderick's lead and handfast to a lovely Scottish lass?"

"'Twould take more than the few minutes we have left before we're missed to tell you the whole of it."

MacInness knew it would a tale worth hearing. "When you've been released, then."

They parted, each with a task that would help MacInness ferret out the truth and the culprit. Walking back would take the rest of his strength, but it had been worth it to meet with Patrick alone—unobserved.

When he reached the postern gate, his steps were slow and his head pounding. His wife was waiting for him. He blinked, but the vision didn't disappear. She stood waiting just outside the gate.

"Lass, what are ye doin' all alone?"

She looked over her shoulder before answering, "I was worried."

MacInness's heart lightened that the lass had taken him at his word and would speak when they were alone. "I'm hard to kill, lass."

Her eyes filled with tears. Did she care for him?

"Where were you?"

While he appreciated her concern for him, he wasn't ready to confide in her as he did his friend. There were things to be sorted through, the very least of which would be finding the man who'd tried to kill him. Then there was the loyalty of the guard…the list seemed endless.

"I needed to clear my head."

She looked as if she wanted to ask more, but the sound of footsteps approaching had her falling silent.

"Come, lass," he said offering his arm. "We've tasks to complete before the evening meal."

⇶✹⇷

GENVIEVE WANTED TO ask Winslow whom he'd left the keep to meet. It was obvious to her he was troubled when he returned. And then there was the flash of something in his eyes that hinted he had something on his mind that troubled him and that he would not be sharing with her.

Could she blame him? The question pricked at her conscience while they walked along the garden path, through the carefully tended herbs and to the door to the kitchens.

If she had hoped for more affection from her husband, she was disappointed. He patted her hand as if she were a cousin—or his sister. "I'll leave ye here, then."

Was he preoccupied with his own troubles, or had his desire for her burned itself out in one night?

When she would have called out to him to ask, Beatrice appeared in the doorway.

"Milady," she said. "We're about to open a cask of wine and need you to oversee the duty."

Her husband nodded, and she noticed the twinge of pain he sought to hide. She might have missed it if she hadn't been studying him so closely. She motioned to Beatrice that she would follow and reached out to her husband.

Winslow looked as if he didn't want to wait, but she wasn't about to give him a choice. "You're in pain."

He looked down at her hand on his arm and then into her eyes. "Ye truly care then, lass?"

She felt her cheeks heat. But she hadn't the time to worry about her reaction to his question. He was her husband and in pain. "Did you think I wouldn't?"

He sighed, but was it because of her words or the sound of them? Mayhap he was hoping for a different answer. She didn't know and right now didn't have the time to pursue it. He shrugged.

"I have an herbal draught that was used to cure my mother's headaches."

"Yer voice doesna sound as rough today."

If his words meant to reassure her, they had the opposite effect. She clamped her mouth shut and shook her head. *Merde*, she had forgotten how she sounded for a moment. Rather than be grateful that she could speak, she worried how it sounded and if she'd ever regain the full use of her voice.

Come, she mouthed.

"Dinna fret about how you sound," he told her.

She ignored his words, and tugged on his hand in answer, pulling him into the kitchens with her. She went right to where she'd left the small supply of herbs, reached for a goblet, filled it with warm water from the pot heating over the cooking fire, and sprinkled a pinch of the ground-herb mix from a small jar.

She stirred it and handed it to her husband.

He hesitated, then took it from her.

The truth hit her like a blow. *Mon Dieu*, he didn't trust her! Had he heard the same rumor she had overheard on her way to the hall this morning, that she had had someone try to kill him?

He didn't know what was in her heart—she hadn't told him. But more, she had no wish to become a widow again.

When he didn't drink from the goblet, she snatched it back and downed half the contents and glared at him.

The taste was the first thing she noticed. It wasn't right. She put a hand to her throat.

"Lass?"

"I—" She felt odd. She walked back over to the alcove and the high shelf where she'd placed her small supply of healing herbs. Reaching for the tiny jar, she opened it and sniffed it.

This wasn't her mix.

"What's wrong?"

The heat radiating from his body warmed her. When had she grown so cold? Her gaze met his and she was suddenly afraid. "Don't drink it."

She was going to pour it on the floor, but he stopped her. "We may need to save this." He took the goblet from her and placed it on the table tucked into the alcove beneath the shelf.

He was speaking, but the rest of his words sounded so far away, indistinct. A tingling sensation pricked at her fingertips and worked its way up her arms as fear iced through her belly.

"Winslow," she wanted to warn him, but the room was growing dim. "I'm sorry," she rasped as her world went black.

Chapter Fourteen

"Anna!" MacInness shouted for the serving woman, relieved when she burst through the door leading to the long passageway to the hall.

"Milord—" Her worried gaze met his and at the ashen face of the woman in his arms.

"What happened?"

He looked over his shoulder. "Somethin' in the herbs she mixed for my achin' head."

Nodding to the goblet on the table he absorbed the ache into his body, ignoring it, concentrating on what he had to tell the woman. "She drank it first."

When Anna tilted her head and looked as if she wanted to ask him why, he continued. "Send yer most trusted servant out the postern gate and stop Patrick, he should be halfway to Merewood Keep by now."

"Patrick?"

"Ye canna miss him," MacInness said. "He stood beside me when I wed—"

"Tall warrior, dark hair, green eyes?"

MacInness nodded. "Tell him there's trouble."

The woman nodded. "What about milady?"

"Do ye have a healer ye trust with yer life?"

Fear flickered in the older woman's eyes, but she nodded.

"Aye, milord."

"Send for her then, and pray we're not too late." The lass had saved his life. Had she meant to kill him and had a change of heart?

Anna moved to the goblet and MacInness ground out, "Dinna touch it." The fear in his wife's eyes and memory of her in his arms weighed heavily toward her innocence.

She stopped and curtseyed. "I'll send Mary to ye."

Striding along the passageway, MacInness prayed. He hadn't spoken to God in years, but he prayed now. "Dinna take her yet. I need her."

By the time MacInness laid Genvieve on their bed, she was so cold. He covered her with a blanket and when she didn't warm, took her back into his arms and sat on the bed.

"Milord?"

"Are ye Mary, then?" He wasn't sure he could trust her, but there wasn't time to question her.

She walked over to where he sat cradling his wife in his arms and asked, "How long has she been like this?"

"Since she drank the headache draught she prepared for me." His heart sank. She was so cold. Did God care or would he snatch the woman away before MacInness could decide if he cared for her or loved her?

"I need to know what's in the herbal mix before I can decide what's to be done."

"I brought milady's jar of herbs," Anna said, holding out the small, round lidded jar.

Mary looked at MacInness. "She'd be more comfortable on the bed."

He shook his head. "Her skin's like ice."

Mary's eyes narrowed as if she were thinking. "Keep her warm then." Taking the jar from Anna she opened it and sniffed. Held it away from her nose and sniffed again.

"That's odd," she said, then mumbled something more beneath her breath.

"I didna hear that last, can ye repeat it?" It sounded like she'd said Witches' Glove. The name didn't bode well.

Mary shook her head. "No time." She put the lid back on the jar and set it into the basket she'd brought with her. Working swiftly the young woman had a brazier carried up and set in the corner of the room.

"What about the smoke?" MacInness didn't think it was wise to light the brazier, the ceiling was too low.

"She needs the heat."

He nodded and didn't question the healer again as she sorted through her supply of herbs and selected and ground out what he hoped would be the cure to bring his wife back.

Through the next hour, he took turns with Anna trying to force the healer's herbal mix down his semi-conscious wife's throat and holding her while her stomach rebelled.

"What now?" MacInness asked as the healer stepped back from the bed.

Genvieve had little or no color, but at least the gray cast to her skin changed and it was now pasty white.

"We wait—and pray."

"There isna anythin' else to be done?" He refused to believe he had to sit and wait for a miracle. He wasn't sure he still believed in them.

"Nay, milord," Mary answered. She sounded weary.

"I've no' thanked ye yet," he said rising from where he'd been sitting on a stool by the bed.

Her gaze met his. "Don't thank me yet, milord," she cautioned. "We need to see if she can be roused, that will tell if she'll waken."

"If?" MacInness thundered. The need to pound something nearly overwhelmed him; he fought to control the urge and won. He spun around and stalked back over to where Mary sat, willing her to speak with every fiber of his being.

Mary closed her eyes and sighed. When she opened them, she met MacInness's direct gaze. "Help me rouse her."

MacInness felt the icy stab of fear slicing through his middle but tamped it down and nodded. "Tell me what to do."

Mary started by pinching the bottom of his wife's foot. He didn't think that would help, but kept his thoughts to himself.

Genvieve flinched and his stomach bottomed out. Mayhap there were still miracles. "Let me try something."

The healer stepped back and MacInness gathered his wife in his arms. He held her to his heart and whispered in her ear. "If ye can hear me, lass, come back to me. I dinna want to lose ye, lass. Please?"

She stirred but didn't open her eyes.

Mary touched his shoulder, but he shook his head. "Can ye leave us for a moment?"

The healer narrowed her gaze at him and looked as if she wanted to say something, but in the end, agreed.

When the door closed, MacInness laid her back on the bed and hoped his idea would work. She'd craved his touch, burned for him, surely that would rouse her. He ran his hands over her shoulders and down to her fingertips, massaging the muscles, coaxing them to respond.

Genvieve's breathing changed. A good sign, that.

Pulling her back into his arms, he leaned her against his chest and then rubbed his hands from the nape of her neck down to the curve of her waist. She stirred against him.

Taking her by the arms, he held her away from him and rasped, "Genvieve, I need ye, lass." Before he could pull her back against him, her eyelids fluttered.

"That's it! Open yer eyes, Love."

Her eyes slowly opened, though he wasn't sure she was fully aware. "Winslow?"

"Aye, lass." His heart began to pound, as the last few hours of worry and tension came to a head. His body trembled but he ignored it, holding her against his heart, not willing to let go.

She mumbled something that he couldn't quite hear. He laid her back down and brought the covers up to her chin. "What did ye say?" he asked, pressing his lips to her forehead.

Genvieve reached out and touched the tip of her finger to the edge of his jaw. "How's your head?"

"Bloody buggerin'—"

Her eyes widened and he clamped his jaw shut.

"It still pains you," she whispered.

"Lass, have ye no memory of what happened to ye?" He'd never forget the way she collapsed in his arms, the ashen cast to her skin, or the terrible fear that she'd die.

Genvieve closed her eyes.

For the second time he wondered, had she intended to give him the draught? Though he cursed that it was there, the niggling suspicion would not go away.

MacInness stood and paced by the bed, the ache in his head and surge of unfamiliar emotions making him daft. His clan would label him as mad as Black Iain.

"Winslow?"

He stopped and turned toward his wife, but didn't speak, afraid of what might pop out of his mouth in his present state of mind.

"Someone tampered with my herbal blend."

He'd thought so as well. Hoped so. Another thought came to mind. "Are ye certain ye didn't add something yerself by accident."

The hurt look flickering in her gray eyes had him wanting to bite off his tongue. The last thing he wanted to do was cause her more pain.

"Yes."

A one-word answer, never a good sign when a woman was involved. *God give me back my simpler life.* As soon as he thought the words, he wanted to take them back. Without Mary's help, he'd almost gotten his wish!

"The healer, Mary, will be by to check on ye."

Genvieve nodded and looked away.

"Dinna fret," he soothed. "Ye can collect more herbs from the garden." He paused and wondered why she still wouldn't look at him. "'Tis vast."

After a pause that had the hair on the back of his neck standing at attention, MacInness placed a hand on her shoulder. She jolted and whipped her head around. The stark fear in her eyes tore at his heart.

The knock on the door startled them both.

"Milord?"

"'Tis Mary," he said. "Let her have a look at ye."

Before he made a fool of himself, blundering by saying any more, MacInness left his wife in Mary's capable hands.

⇛⇚

GENVIEVE WOULD NEVER forget the pain arrowing through her breast at her husband's suggestion that she'd forgotten the simplest of headache remedies. But he didn't know her well, and couldn't possibly know she'd been preparing the cure for her mother for years. Especially after her mother had lost the last babe she carried. Though no longer a young woman, losing a babe had left her mother with a constant pain in her head … and Genvieve suspected one in her heart as well.

"Milady?"

Mary sounded surprised to see her awake. Rather than trust her voice, she put a hand to her throat. Mary nodded as if she just remembered her mistress could not speak. So far Genvieve had only trusted Anna and Beatrice not to gossip about the way her voice sounded. Let everyone else think her mute.

"I didn't think you'd recover so quickly."

Why? she asked, waiting for Mary to follow the movement of her lips.

"The herbal mixture," Mary began. "Witches' Glove, milady?"

Genvieve shivered and pushed herself up in bed. Mary moved

to help her get comfortable.

"Didn't you know?"

Should she risk speaking and thereby becoming the fodder of gossip as she had been at Merewood? She hated the looks of pity. Genvieve shook her head.

"Well then…"

Genvieve reached out to clasp the healer's hand. Mary's gaze met hers. "I've heard Anna and Beatrice talking with one another, and know you can speak when no one else is around to hear you. It doesn't matter what it sounds like. It would save time if you would please speak to me and tell me what you think happened?"

Genvieve tried to pull her hand free, but Mary held fast, giving it a gentle tug. "You think someone tampered with your herbs, don't you?"

She looked away and Mary let go of her hand. Who would have? She barely knew anyone at the holding, hadn't been there more than a few weeks. Who would hate her so? A black thought hit her right between the eyes…whoever wanted Winslow dead.

She turned back and her gaze collided with Mary's. She had to tell someone the horrible suspicion that lanced through her belly, and it would save time if she could just say it one time. "Whoever struck my husband."

Mary's eyes widened, but didn't ridicule the sound of her mistress's voice. Then she nodded. "'Twould make sense. Did you tell him?"

Genvieve frowned, "No."

"Because?" Mary prompted.

"He wouldn't believe me." Sadness engulfed her.

"You hide behind the guise of not being able to speak when you can and you won't tell your husband your suspicions about the herbal remedy," Mary stated baldly. "Either you have something to hide or—"

"I've nothing to hide," Genvieve croaked. Her hand flew to her throat and tears filled her eyes. *Merde.* She sounded pitiful.

Understanding filled the healer's gaze. She sat on the stool beside the bed. "I've a potion or two that would ease your throat."

Genvieve blinked. "Others have tried."

"'Tis the sound that bothers you?"

"My voice is weak, and it sounds like someone is…" She let her voice trail off; it should be obvious to the woman how it sounded.

Mary sighed. "People can be cruel with their words, milady," she said. "But not always their intentions."

Genvieve had wondered about that. For now, she'd not risk being ridiculed.

"What about your husband?"

"I speak when we are in private."

Mary smiled. "You trust him."

She nodded. "With my life."

"But not enough to tell him about the herbs?"

Mary's question had her wondering why she hadn't spoken up when Winslow was in the room with her.

"He'd mentioned it, and I didn't want to place the blame on any of the servants, any one of whom could have added the extra herb to the jar."

Mary's gaze warmed. "Thank you."

Genvieve's throat began to throb, unused to speaking so much. She rubbed at it without thinking.

"I'll mix up something for your throat," the other woman promised, "but I think if your husband rubbed it for you to loosen the muscles, it might feel better faster."

Winslow's hand on her throat brought other images to mind. She felt her face heat.

Mary grinned. "I don't believe you intended to poison your husband."

Poison! The ugly word arrowed through her heart and pounded in her head. Mary had the right of it; when not used to heal, herbs could kill. But who would have tampered with her herbs? Who hated Winslow or herself that much?

Her upper lip beaded with sweat as her heart continued to pound. She grew light headed. Was it the kidnappers, or did someone else want Winslow dead?

Chapter Fifteen

Lady Annaliese tore through her chamber, throwing anything small enough to fit into her hand.

"I told you to kill him, Jacques!"

"But, milady—" the dark knight began.

"No excuses," she seethed. Her plans to ship her daughter back to Normandy were falling apart. First the Scots barbarian rescued her then he married her. It was intolerable!

"How hard can it be to kill someone?" she demanded.

The knight flexed his hands and looked away from her.

She flew across the room and poked him in the chest. "I asked you a question."

He flinched and stepped back. "I…not hard, milady."

"Then do it," she said turning her back on the warrior.

"But he'll suspect—"

She whirled around. "Were my instructions not clear?" she asked, her voice pitched low.

The knight bowed and backed out of the room.

⇶⫷

"What are ye doing out of bed?"

Genvieve flinched, but held her ground, waiting for her husband to catch up to her. She needed to escape the walls of their home for just a little while.

"Walking?" she said, trying to hide the tremor racing up her spine at the sight of Winslow striding toward her, his kilt molding to his powerful thighs. The afternoon breeze blew his glorious red hair away from his handsome face. She couldn't help the sigh that escaped.

"Are ye well enough?"

It was telling that he hadn't referred to her as lass since the other day when she'd offered him a draught for his headache.

They were no closer to discovering who had added the deadly herb to her mix, and she'd taken the precaution of storing her healing herbs in their chamber.

No one entered their chamber, Anna or Beatrice and only when either Winslow or she were present so for now, no one would be able to poison her husband.

"Aye."

When he reached her side, Genvieve started walking again. She really didn't know what to say to her husband. How did one broach the subject of the attempt on one's life without arousing suspicions? She'd heard the rumors and knew what was being said about her.

They walked in silence for another ten minutes before she stopped and turned toward him. "Why don't you just ask me?"

"Ask ye what?" His voice had a rough edge to it. If she hadn't been intimately acquainted with the Scotsman, she'd worry that he was angry with her. As it was, she knew he was worried, not angry.

They'd reached the bend in the road and were halfway to the edge of the forest. Genvieve wished she wasn't concerned with what Sedgeworth's people thought of her or her new husband. From what she'd overheard, their last overlord was a vain, selfish man, only interested in what he could glean from the revenues he owed to the king. It was ultimately that part which he held back that led to his ultimate death.

His intense scrutiny proved to be her undoing as finally, she simply bit out, "Do you think I tried to kill you?"

"I canna say."

Anguish slashed through her middle, flaying her belly wide open. How could he doubt her? Why would he believe her? The need to be alone and think overwhelmed her. Rather than ask permission, as she may have done before she'd been kidnapped, she simply spun about on her heel and strode off without saying a word.

What could she say, anyway? That she would never hurt him? That he was the reason she lived and breathed? That her heart hurt just knowing that Winslow didn't trust her? Each and every thought lanced through her, leaving the wounds to fester.

The heavy footfalls close behind her had Genvieve drawing in a deep breath. He was not going to let this lie. Without turning around, she asked, "If you don't trust me, why haven't you had me locked in our chamber?"

The deep, rumbling chuckle was not the answer she expected. Looking over her shoulder, she frowned at him. "You find this funny?"

"Aye, lass."

Her heart warmed when he called her *lass*. Maybe things were not so bad after all. "Which part, the part where I'm locked in our chamber, or the—"

"'Tis yer temper, lass. It does ye credit."

Before she could steel herself against whatever comment her husband made next, he gripped her shoulders and spun her around. She lost her footing and fell into his arms.

Pushing away from him, she said, "I don't have a temper."

He brushed the tips of his fingers across her brow. Drawing in a steadying breath, she opened her eyes, ready to tell him how much his distrust hurt her. He was waiting for her and dipped his head to capture her lips.

And all thought ceased.

"Winslow," she moaned, need clawing deep inside of her,

struggling to be freed. Desire, hot and potent, raged to the point where she could not control it. Rather than try, she gave in to the glorious feelings coursing through her, heating her to the point of conflagration.

His hands were everywhere at once, molding...seducing. Her body surrendered to his deft but gentle caresses. How had he remembered where to touch and how much pressure to use?

When she felt the breeze caressing the tops of her thighs, she jolted back to awareness. They were standing beside the road, her husband's hands lifting the hem of her bliaut and chainse, and from the look in his eyes, he had no intention of stopping before he'd taken what she desperately wanted to give.

"We can't." She gripped his upper arms, trying to keep him from leaning back down and kissing her senseless again.

"I beg to differ, lass." His mouth curved up on one side as the light of devilment danced in his amber eyes.

Genvieve knew if she didn't do something, he'd be laying her down and making love to her on the soft-packed dirt of the road.

"I'd rather not...here...in the dirt."

Winslow swept her up into his arms and nuzzled the side of her neck. "Dinna think to put me off. I wilna wait for ye."

"But—"

Again, his lips insistently coaxed a reaction from her. She stopped worrying and gave herself over to her husband's commanding touch. The grass beneath her was cool, the trees overhead thick with leaves, but the slumberous gaze boring into hers had her world narrowing to the man poised above her and the feelings only he could rouse.

"Lass, I've been worried about ye," he rasped, trailing a line of kisses along the edge of her jaw and onto her collarbone.

"I thought you were angry."

His lips lingered on a spot just below the hollow at the base of her throat. She shivered.

"I thought I'd lost ye."

"You thought I was trying to poison you," she accused him.

"For an intelligent woman, lass, ye're not very bright."

She drew in a breath, ready to tell him what she thought of him, but never got the chance—his hips ground against hers and the longing pooled low in her belly. The need to join with this man filled her, overwhelming every other need, every other thought.

"Winslow," she breathed out, a whispered prayer. "I love you."

He stiffened, poised to slide into her warmth.

Her heart had spoken, though her head had warned it not to.

Dropping his forehead onto hers, he didn't move until she prodded him. "You don't have to love me back," she told him. Honesty deserved honesty. Though she hadn't planned on confessing what had been blossoming in her heart since the day he'd saved her from certain death. Now that the words had been said, there was no taking them back. As if she would—as if she could.

The longer her husband remained silent, the deeper her worry that he'd never repeat those words to her became. She didn't expect him to, but she'd hoped. Lord, how she'd hoped.

MacInness couldn't think. His mind was muddled with lust, passion, and a healthy dose of fear. Fear that she hadn't meant to say she loved him, and fear that he could never say the words back. If ever a woman deserved to hear them, it was his raven-haired wife.

When he'd succumbed to the feelings rioting inside of him, he couldn't say. He'd thought his heart securely held in the hands of Lady Jillian. But now, looking down into eyes as gray as storm clouds skidding across a Highland sky, he couldn't remember when he had not loved Genvieve.

"'Tis the greatest gift, lass." His voice broke over the words, but it couldn't be helped. "I'll no' do anythin' to make ye regret the givin' of it."

Her hands swept up his sides and curved around to his back, pressing him closer, bringing his mouth down to hers. He followed willingly, letting his lips explore the contours of her mouth fully, penetrating her sweetness with his tongue, then sipping from her lips to savor the richness of her flavor.

A different kind of tasting had him growing hard with desire. "Will ye let me love ye?"

In answer, Genvieve lifted her hips, helping him to slide home in the honeyed warmth his body craved.

He tried to control his thrusts, the pace of them, the depth, but her wild cries of ecstasy snapped his control. Mindless, steeped in the feel of her, the scent of her, MacInness gave himself over to the madness making love to Genvieve had become. When his brain simply shut down, his body took control, dragged them both to the peak of passion, and tossed them over.

Chapter Sixteen

Patrick hailed MacInness as he was saddling his horse.

"I'm no' deaf," he bit out, "just busy."

The Irishman chuckled. "I can see your lovely bride has been softening your rough exterior."

MacInness scowled at him. He'd just left his wife and insisted she rest; she looked so tired to him. He doubted she'd recovered yet from the herbal draught. And that was why he'd asked Patrick to come to Sedgeworth.

He looked at his friend. "Have ye been able to find out anythin'?"

Patrick shook his head and leaned in close. "There's a rumor," he paused. "You won't like it."

MacInness snorted. "I've already heard it."

"Not this one."

MacInness paused and looked at Patrick. The hard look in his friend's eyes decided him. "Come with me, then. I've got to check on the southern perimeter."

They rode in silence until they reached the edge of the woods, then MacInness demanded, "Out with it."

"I heard your lady can speak."

MacInness shrugged. "What of it?"

The Irishman cleared his throat. "Some say it's just a ruse, that she never lost her voice in the first place."

When MacInness remained silent, the other man continued, "A ploy to get you to marry her, and now that she has, she plans to kill you to get the holding and all its revenues."

Shocked to the soles of his well-worn boots, MacInness rode in silence, looking neither to the left nor the right, but straight ahead at the road winding away from them.

"Do you believe it?" Patrick asked.

"Nay. I was there, but too far away, when she received the blow to her throat. The lass was terrified she'd never speak again," he told his friend.

Patrick waited and MacInness said, "I was the one to help her find a way to communicate without words—her relief was real."

"Do you trust her?"

He looked at Patrick and then nodded toward a break in the trees and a stream. They led their horses over to the water.ND Dismounting, MacInness waited while his horse drank his fill.

"I have no reason not to trust her."

"But what about the attack?"

"She wasn't there."

"You looked behind you?"

"No," MacInness held the other man's gaze. "I'd sense if she was there."

Patrick snorted, his derision obvious.

MacInness got in his friend's face and said, "I can tell when she's within ten feet of me."

Patrick raised one eyebrow in silent question.

"'Tis the truth."

"Do you have the sight, then?" his friend demanded.

"If you *maun* know, 'tis her woman's scent."

Patrick nodded. "What about the herbal draught she prepared just for you?"

MacInness rubbed a hand on the back of his neck. "Ye didn't see the hurt in her eyes when I hesitated to take it from her." He swallowed against the lump of emotion clogging his throat. "Then she drank it down and from the confused and shocked expression on her face, I could tell that something was gravely wrong, someone had tampered with the herbs."

"What will you do now?"

Their horses had wandered away from the water and the men collected them, mounted up, and continued on their patrol. MacInness breathed deeply. "I think it all comes back to the day I stumbled upon Genvieve bein' beaten."

Patrick's jaw clenched, and MacInness nodded. "All but one of the bloody bastards died, and I'd be willin' to bet whoever wanted my wife dead then, still does and is tryin' to make it seem as if Genvieve is behind the attempts ta kill me."

"What if it is Genvieve?"

His heart simply stopped, then resumed beating. "It's not."

"You're a good judge of character, MacInness. If you say she's innocent, then we'd best find out who's behind the attempts on your life."

"And hers."

Patrick's eyes widened, as if it had only just occurred to him that two peoples' lives were in danger. "I'll be staying the night, and sending word back to Merewood for reinforcements."

"I thought Kelly was already here."

"Aye, but we need more men that we can trust."

"Some of Garrick's?"

Patrick tilted his head to one side. "And de Chauret's."

"But he's Norman—"

"And I trust him with my life."

"Send word then."

Three hours later, they were riding back through the gate. MacInness was just making his way out of the stable when the messenger caught up with him. Patrick and he exchanged worried glances; the messenger didn't need to speak. The color of his plaid told him it was from his mother's clan.

When he received the missive, he dismissed the carrier, sending him to the kitchens for mead and a meal. As soon as they were alone, he handed the missive to Patrick so he could read it to him.

"It's your mother—"

"Can she no' let me lead me own life?" MacInness grumbled.

Patrick's gaze met his and from the devastated look in his friend's eyes, braced himself for bad news.

"Is she sick, then?"

Patrick shook his head and from the look in his eyes MacInness knew. Sorrow cut through his middle like a hot knife through butter. "When did she die?"

"A fortnight ago…'twas a fever."

MacInness appreciated the brief telling, he didn't think he could have handled a long-winded explanation. "And me sisters?"

"They'll not leave their husbands' clans."

He nodded, accepting the news. "Who sent the missive?"

"Garrick's brother."

"Roderick."

"Aye," Patrick answered.

"Is he coming home with his new bride?"

Again Patrick answered in the negative.

Braced, MacInness accepted his response. "I have to go to them."

Patrick nodded. "Shall I wait for you to speak with Lady Genvieve?"

"*Och*, no," MacInness said. "I canna wait."

"Then leave her a note—"

"Ye know I canna write nor read."

Patrick followed MacInness across the bailey and up the steps to the hall, pausing to call out to one of the servants. "I need to send word to Garrick of Merewood and leave a message for Lady Genvieve."

While MacInness took the steps to the upper level two at a time, Patrick penned a note to Genvieve, and another to Garrick, telling of the news from the Highlands and urging Garrick to send someone over to guard Lady Genvieve while they were away.

Ten minutes later, they were gone.

GENVIEVE PAUSED IN her measuring to ask Mary's opinion, when Beatrice burst into the kitchens.

"Milady! I've bad news," the servant said.

Genvieve's heart began to pound. *Lord, don't let it be Winslow.* She nodded, urging Beatrice to speak.

"His lordship's mother has died."

A deep ache swept up from her toes, Genvieve clutched her belly, wrapping her arms about herself to hold in the hurt. "Did they say how?" she rasped.

The servant nodded. "A fever."

She closed her eyes and said a silent prayer for Winslow's mother's soul. "I have to go to him."

"He's gone, milady."

The ache in her belly widened. "Gone?"

"Patrick left a missive for you." Beatrice handed it to her.

"But Winslow didn't?"

"No, milady."

Mary reached out a hand to her, but Genvieve shook her head and brushed past her, hoping to hide the hurt that enveloped her entire being. She'd misunderstood her husband's words. He cared for her out of duty, nothing more. He didn't trust her, or he didn't care. Both were reasons not to tell her of his urgent need to go home.

THREE DAYS LATER, Eamon arrived from the Highlands and all hell broke loose.

Her hands trembled as she motioned for Garrick to have Eamon repeat what he'd just said.

The younger man stared at her as if she had lost her mind, but Garrick urged him to speak.

"MacInness's mother isn't dead."

She placed her hand on the tabletop, bracing herself, before looking at Garrick. *Why?* she mouthed.

"Why what?" he asked.

Did he lie, she exaggerated the words so the two men could understand the movement of her mouth. Her heart was breaking, and she couldn't control the tremors coursing through her at the thought of her handsome husband leaving without saying goodbye, and worse lying about where he was going.

"MacInness never lies," Eamon bit out.

Garrick nodded.

Genvieve's eyes filled with tears, and she desperately blinked them away. She could not break down in front of these men. Later, when she was alone that would be acceptable. Not now.

"How well do you know MacInness?" Eamon asked her.

Garrick intervened, "Lady Genvieve's throat was injured, and it has yet to heal...she has difficulty speaking."

The younger warrior narrowed his eyes but didn't contradict what his overlord was saying. Genvieve didn't know if she should be grateful or not.

Recognizing the look and knowing she would have to accept his reaction to the sound of her voice, she spoke, "Where is he?"

Eamon's expression told her it had not improved by not using it. She still sounded like a scalded cat.

Garrick went to her then, braced a hand around her, and led her over to a chair. Once she was seated, he knelt in front of her. "I don't know," he confessed. "But I promise you, we'll find him."

"And Patrick," she urged, ignored the way he winced.

Garrick slowly stood. "Aye. Rest your voice, it must pain still pain you to speak."

Eamon still hadn't moved, and when his brother Kelly poked him, he walked over to where Genvieve sat. "Are you certain you don't know where your husband is, milady?"

Kelly shoved him into a chair. "I thought you were going to ask if they'd found the bastard who clubbed MacInness from behind."

Eamon caught himself and would have shoved back at his

brother, but Garrick stepped in between them.

"Enough."

"Will it be enough when we find MacInness and Patrick with their throats slit ear to ear?"

Genvieve's stomach roiled and a noxious taste filled her mouth. She shot to her feet, clamped a hand over her mouth and ran out of the hall.

Garrick found her in the corner of the herb garden and held her through the worst of it, offering her a linen square to wipe her mouth when she sat back on her heels.

"Eamon's been in the Highlands too long," Garrick explained. "He never used to speak like that in front of a lady."

She didn't care about that. Since they were alone, she risked speaking aloud, asking, "Do you think that's what happened?" With every ounce of willpower she possessed, she prayed it wasn't true.

Garrick didn't wince this time hearing her speak, and did not answer right away. Finally, he sighed. "No. I think there is more here than we have been told and have yet to find out."

"Who would be so cruel as to send such a missive?"

"Someone who knew MacInness would react the way he did and head off without waiting to discuss it with anyone."

"Except Patrick," she added.

"Patrick O'Malley has been vassal to MacInness for years," Garrick told her. "They've saved one another's lives countless times over."

"What about Kelly and Eamon?"

"They're cousins to Patrick and Sean."

"Who's Sean?" she asked, slowly getting to her feet with Garrick's help.

"Patrick's brother."

"I see."

Garrick shook his head. "I don't think you do. MacInness heads up his Irish Contingent, and they, along with my wife, were instrumental in helping my youngest brother escape from certain death at the hands of the former Lord of Sedgeworth Keep."

As Garrick relayed the events leading up to and immediately following his brother's capture, Genvieve began to understand the unbreakable connection between Winslow and the men and why Lady Jillian and her husband shared a similar bond. She wasn't jealous, but she wasn't comfortable with it either.

"And despite how my husband feels about your wife, you trust him?" she asked.

Garrick's jaw hardened, then relaxed. "I owe him my life and hers, twice over."

"You trust him." He hadn't said as much, but she sensed it instinctively.

He nodded. "But you're mistaken if you think he doesn't care for you, Lady Genvieve."

She wished it were so, but wouldn't count on it.

"Wait here," he said, leading her over to a bench near the steps. "I'll bring you some water."

Genvieve needed the time to think. After reacting to the image Eamon so brutally painted, she searched her heart and her soul and knew Winslow was not dead. All she had to do now was find out what happened and where he was.

When Garrick returned, he handed her the water.

She thanked him and drank deeply. The cool water eased the pain in her throat. "May I accompany you on your search?"

He started to refuse, but for some reason relented. Genvieve wondered if it had to do with the story he'd told her about Lady Jillian following after Garrick to London to try to bargain with the king in order to secure her family's former holding for her husband.

"Can you be ready to leave in an hour?"

"Aye and I'll ask Mary for some healing herbs and poultices and pack some bandages."

"I didn't say that MacInness was hurt."

"You didn't have to."

"I think people underestimate you, Lady Genvieve."

She felt the corner of her mouth lift. "Most do."

"MacInnes wouldn't."

The ache arrowing through her reaffirmed her belief that he was still alive. She embraced it. "No," she whispered. "He wouldn't."

>>>><<<<

MacInnes opened his eyes and swore. The pain slicing through his head nauseated him. He closed his eyes and tried to move and realized his hands were bound behind him, inhibiting his movement. Wherever he was, given his current circumstances, he doubted they were friends.

A loan moan off to the left of him had his eyes snapping open again. The dark shape took the form of the head of his Irish Contingent—Patrick.

"Dinna tell me they got the both of us?" he rasped.

"*Bollocks!* What hit me?"

"Not what, mon. Who." MacInnes had sensed they were being followed and had been preparing for the ambush when he and Patrick were attacked from behind.

"All right then, you damned Scot," Patrick said, "who hit me?"

He snorted, "Damned if I know."

"Then why did you have me ask you?" Patrick groaned.

"I thought it would help pass the time while I figure out how to loosen me bonds."

The other warrior sounded as if he were choking.

"Are ye all right, mon?"

In answer he groaned.

"Does yer head pain ye as well?"

"Aye."

"Like as not, we were both felled from behind." MacInnes wished he'd caught a glimpse of who'd hit them, but it had happened too fast. His gut told him it was all connected with the last two attempts on his life...nay; make that one attempt on his life, and one on Genvieve's.

"Can you move closer?" Patrick asked.

MacInness shifted onto his back, taking deep gulping breaths. The pain in his head was blinding. Once the sensation passed, he sidled over next to his friend.

"Roll onto your side," MacInness said. "I'll try to loosen your bonds first."

It was slow going; he had to stop and breathe slowly to control the constant roiling in his gut.

"Let me try," Patrick offered after several unsuccessful attempts.

MacInness finally admitted defeat and let the other man try to untie the knots. In a matter of minutes, MacInness felt the rope loosen. Rolling over onto his hands and knees he gave in to his body's clamoring need and retched until all that was left were dry heaves.

"Are you done, yet?" Patrick asked quietly.

"Aye," MacInness said. "Though me head still aches."

"Untie me."

"After I toss some straw over this, else the smell will have me losin' the rest of me stomach linin'."

When Patrick was free, they began to look for a way out. After an exhaustive search, they agreed, there was only one way in and one way out of the dank cell they were locked in.

"Someone will be by to check on us sooner or later," Patrick said.

"Who do ye think attacked us?" MacInness had a few guesses, but was interested in what his vassal thought.

"Probably no one we know."

"And why do ye say that?" MacInness wondered how Patrick arrived at that conclusion.

"Because everyone who knows us loves us."

MacInness grunted.

"And if they don't," Patrick added, "they should."

Chapter Seventeen

From what little she'd overheard waiting for Garrick and his men to assemble, there were signs of a small battle on the road north, not five miles from Sedgeworth's front gate. Genvieve wished she'd lived in the area longer. If this had occurred back home, she would have known who to ask for help, who to post as guards, and who to trust at her back.

Her hands trembled as she held the reins more securely in her grasp.

"Are you sure you don't want one of us to accompany you, milady?" Anna's suggestion was a good one, but she was afraid to leave someone she didn't know in charge of the holding in her absence.

She shook her head. "I trust you and Beatrice to look out for our people while I'm gone."

Her voice grated on her nerves, but for once, she didn't care who heard her and what they said about it.

"What about Mary?" Anna asked.

"Is there anyone else who could act as healer in her place?"

Anna shook her head.

Genvieve wouldn't leave them without their healer. Accidents happened, on a daily basis, and she knew the smithy's wife was close to her time.

"We can't let Jean have her baby without Mary's help."

Though she wouldn't mind having Mary accompany her.

"What about Kelly?"

"Have I met her?"

"You've met me," a deep voice answered.

Genvieve looked up and nearly swallowed her tongue. The man was huge, and had a black look on his face. "I have?"

"Aye," he insisted walking his horse over to where she stood with the women.

Merde. She remembered when she'd met him. "You came to help Mary when I…"

She let her words trail off, not wishing to bring up with subject of the attempted murder when the killer was still at large.

Kelly bent down and grabbed a hold of her hand. "You mustn't doubt The MacInness; he's a force to be reckoned with all by himself."

Her throat tightened, so she nodded.

"Besides," he said, dropping her hand, "he has me cousin with him." Kelly's horse started to prance and moved closer to Genvieve, nudging into her.

She moved to the side so the horse wouldn't knock her off her feet. "I thought Eamon was your cousin."

Kelly petted his horse's neck in rhythmic movements to calm him. "Eamon's me brother, Sean and Patrick are our cousins."

"And all of you are O'Malleys, part of the group that used to report to Garrick?" Genvieve hoped she finally had the story straight, but doubted it. There were so many new names and faces to learn, now that she was Mistress of Sedgeworth.

"You truly aren't trying to make your voice sound like someone was killing a cat," Kelly asked. "Are you?"

The heat suffusing her cheeks must have been answer enough, the warrior apologized. "I meant no disrespect, milady."

She shrugged.

"Don't stop talking just because you sound like a…"

She glared at him, waiting for him to finish his statement. When it was clear Kelly wouldn't, she motioned for him to watch her lips and asked him if he was indeed as talented a healer as Mary.

It took three tries for him to read her lips, but finally, he answered her. "Aye, but I've had more experience with the type of wounds MacInness and Patrick are liable to have."

Her stomach cramped and a desperate need to hold onto something solid enveloped her.

As if he knew why she was asking, Kelly leaned down and whispered, "There was a lot of blood spilled."

Tears welled up and flowed over before she realized she was crying.

Kelly's shocked expression didn't make her feel better. "You care?"

I married him, she mouthed.

"Can you move your lips just a bit slower, milady?" he asked. "I didn't understand you."

"Kelly!"

"Over here, Garrick!" he answered the summons.

When the other man joined them, he still refused to move from where he stood in front of Genvieve. "Say that last bit again."

Genvieve wanted to smack the man in the head with something hard. He'd insulted her and now expected her to repeat what she'd very carefully told him twice already?

"Is there a problem, Lady Genvieve?" Garrick asked looking back and forth between them.

She decided to rest her voice. Mayhap she had used it too much and would be ruining it. Mayhap it would never heal. That thought had ice sluicing through her veins. Winslow would always know when his wife was in the room; even if the man were blind, the screeching would surely give her away.

She hugged Anna and then Beatrice and mounted her horse.

"Kelly, you'd best not upset MacInness's bride," Garrick warned.

The other warrior had the audacity to snort and then laugh.

As the men mounted and waited for the rest of their party to do the same, Garrick grumbled, "This is no laughing matter. MacInness will have my head and yours if you upset his wife."

Genvieve watched the byplay between the warriors, but didn't say anything. Her mind wandered while she wondered what they fed these men from birth that had them standing a full head taller than her father or her first husband.

"Apparently, my being here is reason enough to upset the woman," Kelly mumbled.

"Lady Genvieve," Garrick bit out. "It's Lady—"

"I know," Kelly answered before turning to her. "I beg your pardon, milady."

She didn't quite know what to do about Kelly. He seemed to be having trouble looking at her. Had her voice been so horrible sounding that he couldn't look at her without laughing?

A half hour later, she stopped wondering.

"I didn't mean to upset you, Lady Genvieve," he said pulling up alongside her to ride with her, their horses' steps perfectly in time with one another.

She grunted, still not feeling a warmth of forgiveness toward the man. Three hours later, she'd changed her mind.

The attack surprised them all. Arrows were flying at them from all directions.

"Kelly," Garrick shouted. "Protect Lady Genvieve!"

"Milady," Kelly's hoarse shout had her concentrating on the sound of his voice instead of the panic welling up inside of her as a second volley of thin shafts of wood followed the first. He dove off his horse with his arms out in front of him. One wrapped around her and the other broke their fall as the two of them hit the ground with him on top of her.

She heard a faint crack and felt her ribs give way, but she'd cut out her tongue before she said a word as the pike protruding from the tree beside her horse—right where she had been seconds before—wobbled. Taunting her. She'd be dead if not for Kelly.

Genvieve tried to draw in a breath, but couldn't, and didn't know if it was because of her ribs or the weight of the warrior protecting her with his body. When he jolted, she knew he'd been injured.

Pushing out from under him, she demanded, "Tell me where you're hurt."

"Don't move," the warrior ground out, pulling himself back as if to cover her again. But before he could, the battle cries died as suddenly as they had begun.

Genvieve looked around her then and could not believe the carnage. Bodies lay at odd broken angles, littering the ground between where she and Kelly sat and where Garrick stood, his sword dripping with blood.

A young Norman knight made his way over to where she sat holding her ribs, but she didn't recognize him.

"Lady Genvieve," he offered his hand, but she shook her head.

"Don't you trust me?" he sounded incredulous at the very idea.

"It's not that," she said, hoping no one would notice how short of breath she sounded. "Kelly's hurt."

"Aimory," Garrick called out, "see what you can do for Kelly."

"And for Lady Genvieve," Kelly ground out. "I hit her harder than I meant to."

She tried to smile. "You did what you had to."

He grimaced and that's when she noticed the arrow protruding from his shoulder. "Oh, Kelly!"

"We've got to see if we can find out where they came from," another man called out and Garrick nodded. "Aimory, see to them both."

But Genvieve was already ripping the bottom of her bliaut to help staunch the flow of bright red blood from the warrior's shoulder. So much blood from such a thin shaft of wood. Her hands trembled as she pressed the fabric around the arrow.

Aimory went to Kelly's horse, grabbed the satchel and brought it over to where she and the other warrior were sitting. Her knees were caked with mud, but she didn't give it more than a passing thought because all of her energy was focused on breathing in and out while stopping the bleeding.

"We don't have time to remove the arrow now," Aimory told her. "We'll wait until we are safe."

Kelly groaned, and she realized the news would not be welcomed by either of them. She hurt for the Irishman. When she started to rise to her feet, something shifted inside of her, making her head light and the ground spin.

"Easy," someone said, bracing her against him. The last thing she would remember was the lovely cadence of the man's voice.

She came to when someone was prodding her side. Her moan of pain had the dark-haired man stopping to look at her. "Yer awake then, lass?"

"Winsl—" She shook her head. "Not Winslow." And the man definitely was not, but he was Scottish. "Do I know you?" she asked.

He tilted his head to one side and finally shrugged. "I canna say."

She closed her eyes, missing the lilting sound of her husband's voice. He'd been gone for days.

"Dinna greet for the mon, he's no' dead yet," the voice told her.

Genvieve remembered her husband telling her not to greet, to cry, once before. But he wasn't here. She slowly opened her eyes and let them focus on the man who had ceased to prod her aching ribs, but was instead now reaching for her bliaut as if to lift it off of her. She pressed a hand in between her breasts and shook her head.

"But ye've hurt yer ribs, lass," he said. "I need to be wrappin' them."

"I'm not going to take off my clothes off in front of all of these men." Her voice cracked and squeaked, but not one of the men showed a reaction to the sound of it.

"Iain!" Garrick shouted, "What's keeping you?"

"Lady Genvieve," he answered. "She won't let me take care of her ribs."

"What's wrong with her ribs," Garrick asked, walking toward them.

"Nothing," she lied.

"Cracked," Iain answered at the same time, with a nod in her direction.

"MacInness isn't going to be happy with you, Kelly," Garrick predicted.

"Oh, milady," Kelly began, "I'm sorry."

"You didn't do it on purpose."

He laughed, then groaned, as the movement shifted the arrow in his shoulder. "True, but to ensure your safety, I'd probably do it again," he said, rising to his feet.

"Iain," Kelly said, "I've got a length of clean, thin linen in my satchel, you can wrap it around her bliaut, so she only has to remove her chainse."

"What *guid* will that do the lass?" the Scotsman demanded.

"Until we get to a safer place, her ribs will be immobile," Kelly said, "especially if we make her promise not to move unless we tell her to."

Genvieve hated being spoken to as if she wasn't there. "I will most definitely move." She shifted, and saw stars, as her ribs flexed where they'd broken.

"Are ye sure, then, lass?"

She sighed. "What do you need me to do?"

"I'm going to slice off yer outer garment so ye don't have to lift yer arms, or remove yer under garment."

Having trouble drawing in a breath, she whispered her thanks.

In a matter of moments, her bliaut was ripped beyond repair, but the warrior was wrapping the length of linen around her aching ribs. Bound and immobile, she did feel a little better.

"Who do you think did this?" she asked, watching the men help Kelly to his feet and up onto his horse.

"I have a few suspicions," Garrick said. "But will need your cousin to confirm them."

Later that night, she would wonder why Augustin would have the answers.

⇛⇚

"Do you think they've forgotten about us?"

MacInness shrugged. "I dinna know."

"How's your head?"

"How do ye think it is?" MacInness bit out. He was deeply worried. Who had attacked them and why? But more, was Genvieve safe at home? Was there more of a plot afoot than they'd realized?

Patrick nudged him with his shoulder and MacInness grumbled, "Dinna start."

Patrick nudged him again and MacInness chuckled. "If me head didn't feel like I'd split it open again, I could take ye down, mon."

"I'd like to see you try."

"*Aneuch*," MacInness said. "I think the bastards hit me in the same spot on the back of me head."

"No wonder you were seeing double and puking up your guts."

MacInness didn't really need the reminder; he remembered the humiliating way he'd been on his hands and knees just hours before. Patrick was a friend, but like as not, would repeat what had happened to more than just his cousins and, the next time he saw him, his brother.

Far too many people for MacInness's liking, but it couldn't be helped.

A sound echoed from what had to be a long passageway.

"Did ye hear that?"

Patrick stood and pulled MacInness with him. He wobbled, but found his balance.

"Well then, they've finally decided to pay us a visit, laddie."

Patrick cocked his head to one side, listening. "I think we should welcome them, when they come to call."

MacInness chuckled. "Aye, me mother, God rest her soul, would be proud of ye."

The men lowered their voices and had the plan before the keys jingled just outside their door indicating their visitors had arrived.

The door swung open. "Get up you lazy Scot!" a deep voice shouted.

MacInness didn't move, but he moaned for effect.

"You too, Irish bastard!" a second voice ground out.

Patrick grunted when someone kicked him, but he didn't move either.

"Do you think we hit them too hard?" the one man asked the other.

"Maybe we've saved Lady Annaliese the trouble of having him killed."

"Shut your trap!" the deep voice ground out.

"They aren't awake, and can't hear us," the other man answered.

"We aren't to take any chances until we have Lady Genvieve back where her mother wants her."

MacInness's stomach threatened to rebel on the spot. Her mother was behind the attack and abduction?

"What does she have planned for her daughter?"

"You don't want to know."

The chill of those words raced up MacInness's spine, leaving him light headed. Her own mother had plotted against her! He could not conceive of it. He'd just learned he'd lost his mother and now he was going to have to lie to his wife and tell her she'd lost hers as well. It would be far kinder than the truth that

Genvieve's mother plotted to have him killed and who knew what the woman planned to do to her daughter.

He tensed and cracked his knuckles, twice. As one, he and Patrick shot to their feet and overpowered their captors. MacInness smiled as they pummeled the men and then cracked their heads together.

"Not very hardheaded," he mumbled to Patrick. "It only took one crack. Most Scots or Irish would take at least two or three cracks against another man's skull before they'd lost consciousness."

"Aye," Patrick agreed. "They must be Normans."

Using the length of leather that had bound their hands behind their backs earlier, MacInness and Patrick tied the men up and made their way down the passageway to freedom.

Chapter Eighteen

"I don't want to look at him," Genvieve insisted. She looked over her shoulder at the man leaning against the trunk of a tree with the arrow between his eyes.

"Dinna mind the blood, lass." Iain warned her.

"I wouldn't ask," Garrick said, "if we didn't need you to see if you could identify him."

His jaw was tight with what she knew was suppressed anger. Anger that they'd been attacked and that three of the attackers had escaped during the fray.

The look on Garrick's face changed as he leaned in close. "The longer you put it off, the longer Kelly will have to wait to have the arrow removed."

Her hands flew to her mouth, and she struggled to calm her roiling stomach. "I'm sorry," she rasped. "Of course, I'll look at the man."

Garrick reached out and placed his hand beneath her elbow and guided her over to the fallen attacker. She shivered once, and felt the bile rising in her queasy stomach, but clamped her jaw shut tight and dug deep for a courage she didn't feel. The arrow protruded from the middle of the man's forehead and blood still dripped in rivulets into the man's sightless eyes.

Closing her eyes to gather her fleeting courage, she breathed deeply. The hand on her elbow swept around to her back. She leaned against Garrick's strength, grateful that he understood she needed his support—just for a moment.

When she opened her eyes, she was ready. Ignoring the blood, looking past it to the man beneath, she concentrated on the shape of the man's face and the size of him. A flicker of a memory from her interrupted journey to accompany her young cousin Angelique to join her father at Merewood Keep had her seeing double.

Literally. There had been two men, twins, in the party of warriors who were to escort her on to her ailing mother, rather than the planned trip north to Merewood Keep. The dead man before her was one of the brothers.

She swayed as another memory assaulted her, this one of the nightmare abduction and the man who'd delivered the blow that had rendered her temporarily mute—the dead man's brother.

"Do you recognize the mon, lass?"

She nodded. "His name's Jean and his brother is Claude. They were part of my mother's private guard."

Iain and Garrick looked at one another and then back at Genvieve. She didn't want to go into the details now, but she did for the sake of one man. Winslow MacInness. She wanted to find her husband. Needed to find him and tell him she remembered what happened. He was in grave danger, for she had just remembered the name the kidnappers had let slip before she tried to escape and they beat her—Annaliese de Chauret...her mother!

The party rode in silence and Genvieve didn't ask where they were headed. She'd thought they would set up camp for the night, but they rode past one clearing after another. Too heartsick to approach Garrick and ask why their plans had changed, she kept her back as straight as possible so as not to injure her ribs further, vowing to seek her cousin out as soon as possible.

She felt every dip and bump in the road. Genvieve didn't want to complain, but the pain tearing through her had tears blurring her vision. A quick look to the left told her that the warrior riding alongside her wasn't paying any attention to her.

She used the edge of her sleeve to wipe her eyes and struggled to breathe.

"Do ye need to stop, then?"

She nearly jumped out of the saddle. "I...er...no," she lied.

The Scotsman's sigh was deep and heartfelt. "Yer no' a *guid* liar, milady."

Garrick was beside her before she could respond. "I should have realized it would be too painful to ride this distance, Lady Genvieve."

She wanted to tell him it was all right and that she could ride for as long as she had to, but he leaned over toward her, wrapped an arm around her and gathered her to his massive chest. "Rest," he ordered, one hand securely around her and the other on the reins.

The heat from his body warmed her, relaxing her to the point where she closed her eyes. Just for a minute, she promised herself.

Genvieve woke as they were approaching Merewood Keep's curtain wall. The warriors calling out to Garrick had her struggling to wipe the sleep from her eyes. "I thought we were going to search for my husband."

Garrick's jaw was clenched, still he spoke, "We are."

"But—"

"I believe your cousin will be able to help us locate MacInness and Patrick."

The huge log securing the gate was lifted and the gate swung inward, allowing Garrick and his warriors to enter the bailey. Genvieve wanted to insist that she could dismount on her own, but Garrick shook his head and handed her off to Armand, another of her cousin's men.

"Milady," he rasped, holding her securely in his arms, "what happened?"

"Later," Iain bit out, helping Kelly dismount. "Take us to de Chauret."

Armand paused, but one look from Garrick and the younger

warrior strode across the bailey and up the steps to the hall. The first person Genvieve saw was her cousin's daughter.

"Genvieve!" her glad cry echoed in the sudden silence.

Looking over her shoulder, Genvieve realized just how bedraggled and bloody their group was.

"Maman," Angelique called out, "we need your healing herbs."

Lady Eyreka paused and called out to one of the serving women instructing her to fetch the healing herbs and her supply of clean strips of linen. "What happened?"

Armand set Genvieve on the nearest bench and went back to help the wounded into the hall.

"Are you sure you want to stay and help?" Genvieve asked the little girl, her voice still rough.

Augustin nodded, seemingly pleased that even though her voice sounded horrible, she was speaking. "My daughter helped save my lady wife's life, did I not have an opportunity to tell you?"

Genvieve shook her head and immediately regretted the action.

Eyreka's knowing look didn't bother her. She felt abysmal and didn't know how much longer she was going to be able to hold out, waiting for Kelly to be taken care of. If she could just have something for the pain in her head.

The cup appeared before her almost as she finished making the wish. She didn't hesitate, trusting Lady Eyreka not to want to do her harm, she drank deeply. Almost immediately the pain over her left eye eased, but it was probably because she knew the herbal draught would work.

"Let me help with Kelly," she insisted, but no one listened to her, instead they settled the Irishman onto a bench, while Garrick heated the blade they would use to seal the injury once they extracted the arrow shaft.

"I can—"

"Be quiet," Iain said, coming to stand beside her.

"Of all the arrogant, pigheaded..."

"You *maun* want to stop there, lass," Iain said.

"You'll turn his pretty head with all your sweet words," Eamon said, looking at her for the first time without rancor.

She wondered what had changed the man's opinion of her, but at the moment was too worried about Kelly to wonder. She stood, Iain reached out as if to stop her, but she said, "Please? He's hurt because of me."

Iain nodded and she walked over to where Kelly sat. Without asking permission, she grabbed a hold of his hand and held tight. All through the arduous process of removing the shaft from his shoulder, she held tight. Her stomach roiled, her heart pounded double-time, and tears trickled into the corners of her mouth, but she didn't let go or look away from the grim set of Kelly's mouth.

"I'd rather it had been me—"

"And I'm certain MacInness will be grateful it wasn't," Kelly answered, locking gazes with her.

"But—"

"'Tis a paltry wound," he said, then sucked in a breath as the shaft slid free.

She moved closer when Lady Eyreka reached for the heated knife. "This will be painful, Kelly," the older woman warned.

"I've used the method myself, many times," Kelly rasped as the sizzle of burning flesh and his soft groan of agony filled the hall.

"I used to think the process of sewing a wound back together was nothing of great import," Lady Eyreka said. "That is, until it was my turn to have a wound stitched back together."

Kelly didn't speak, but he managed to nod.

Genvieve prayed the entire time they worked on him. By the time his wound had been covered with a thick layer of salve, and a bandage applied, she was so tired her eyes burned.

"Your turn, lass." Iain said without missing a beat.

"I don't need—"

"Your ribs, milady," Iain said. "Dinna tell me they've miraculously healed themselves?"

Lady Eyreka's smile eased some of the tension in the hall as she took over Genvieve's care. "If someone will fetch Lady Jillian, I'll need her help upstairs."

The order for more heated water followed them upstairs to the solar.

Jillian joined them just as they were helping Genvieve out of her ragged chainse.

"It'll help if you sit very still," Jillian suggested.

"Have you ever had a cracked rib?"

Jillian nodded, "Yes. Several."

Genvieve fell silent then and let them wash the dust of the journey away and bind her ribs. She could still breathe, so she didn't feel she could complain at how tightly they wrapped the linen around her.

After another herbal draught, she was ready to fall asleep, but fought the need. "I need to find Winslow," she said to the two women.

"Winslow is very resourceful," Jillian said.

"And not to be underestimated," Eyreka added.

"But he doesn't know what he's up against. I've only just realized who is behind the attempts on his life." Her voice broke and her with it her heart.

The women didn't speak, but watched and waited.

"My mother."

Their identical reaction didn't ease the guilt she was feeling. "If it weren't for me, Winslow wouldn't be held captive," she said.

"But he could already have escaped by now," Jillian offered.

"Or been injured," Genvieve whispered, remembering what Iain and Garrick had said about the dried blood they'd found on the plants and ground.

A devastating thought lanced through her. "He wouldn't have had to marry…"

Jillian got up and walked over to sit beside her. "It was for the best," she reassured her. "And Winslow loves you."

"How can you say that," Genvieve asked, "when he still loves you?"

Jillian's eyes flared with emotion, but she didn't back down. "'Tis you he loves, Genvieve," she said quietly. "I was here when he carried your battered body in through the gate."

"He doesn't."

Eyreka sat on the other side of Genvieve and laid a hand on her arm. "He does," she said simply. "You have to trust us, we've known Winslow longer than you have."

Genvieve's heart lurched. Could it be true? Did her husband really love her? He desired her, lusted for her she knew, but love?

A commotion in the hall below then had the women all rising to their feet. As the cry went up, her heart began to thrum a steady beat. Winslow! She couldn't say exactly how she knew, but she sensed her husband had returned.

"Genvieve!" his shout rattled the goblet and bowl on the table. And then the man himself burst through the doorway, blood dripping from a cut high on his forehead and another across his chin.

"Winslow," she rose slowly, carefully and walked toward him. "You're all right?" she asked, knowing he was, yet crying uncontrollably because she thought she'd lost him.

"Dinna greet, lassie," he said as he gathered her to his heart. The dam burst and sobs tore through her body as the fear she'd been holding at bay for the last few days slammed into her with a vengeance.

"You're hurt," she heard Jillian say.

"Ye should see the other mon," her husband rumbled in reply.

He shifted Genvieve in his arms, and she lost her breath, bracing herself against him, she tried to catch it.

"Where are ye hurt, lass?"

The worry in his voice soothed the sharp edge off the pain and allowed her to draw in a breath.

"Her ribs," Eyreka answered. "It was an accident when Kelly threw himself on top of her."

Her husband stiffened, his arms like steel bands around her. "Arrows were being fired from all directions at once," she said, hoping to ease some of the tension in Winslow.

"He didna have to break yer ribs."

Genvieve pushed out of his arms. "Aye," she readily agreed. "He could have left me atop my horse and let the pike aimed at my heart have me."

The tremors coursing through Winslow had her wishing she'd told him slowly, or more carefully.

"I need to sit down." He sat, pulling her onto his lap.

She went willingly. When the door to the solar closed, she didn't look up. Nothing mattered right now except the two of them, right here, right now.

"What happened to you, Winslow?"

He shook his head. "Give a mon a moment, lass."

She waited a few longer than that and then prodded him. "Why didn't you leave me a note to tell me where you'd gone?"

"Patrick knew where I was headed."

"But what about me?" Genvieve demanded.

He brushed a strand of hair off her forehead. "I'm verra sorry to have hurt ye, lass."

"But—"

"Let it go for now, lass," he asked.

She agreed for the moment, vowing to find out why tomorrow.

CHAPTER NINETEEN

MacInness vowed to get to the bottom of the troubles surrounding his new wife and her bitch of a mother without Genvieve finding out, if at all possible. But from the way the lass had taken to following him everywhere, he didn't think he'd have a moment's peace until she closed her eyes.

De Chauret approached him early the next morning. "Do you know what happened?" the older man demanded.

"Aye," he answered. "And I know why."

One eyebrow raised in question was all MacInness needed to reinforce his first reaction. "If I tell ye, ye'll have to promise not to tell the lass."

Augustin walked over to where MacInness sat before the brazier. "Not to tell her what?"

"That I know who was behind her kidnappin'." The heaviness in his chest was spreading down to where his gut ached. The lass wouldn't be taking the news well, and already he dreaded the telling of it.

Augustin signaled for something to drink and eat. While they broke their fast, MacInness filled him in on what he and Patrick had overheard while they were being held captive and the bits and pieces he'd heard when Genvieve was having one of her nightmares.

When Garrick walked into the room, he joined the men and

then proceeded to fill MacInness in on what had happened to them and Genvieve's revelation after identifying one of the attackers.

"It seemed to jar her memory and bring missing fragments back," he said.

"What can we do?" MacInness knew what he wanted to do. He would kill the lying bitch for trying to bring harm to her daughter, the most loving, giving person he'd met since giving up on his quest to make Lady Jillian change her mind and marry him instead of Garrick. Although why he thought of that just now or used it as a comparison he didn't know.

Genvieve walked into the room, her sleek midnight hair brushed against her waist as she made her way over toward them. All other thoughts flew from his mind, leaving every one he had centered on the woman slowly walking toward him.

The men rose to their feet and MacInness demanded, "Why have ye left yer sickbed?"

"I could ask the same of you, husband," she said, coming to a stop right in front of him. With her head tilted back all the way, her hair brushed the backs of her knees, tempting him to reach out and wrap it around the both of them. That thought led to another, one that involved cream colored skin, soft as a new rose, and dewy sweet lips.

Garrick elbowed him in the ribs, getting his attention. "Why have you?"

"Have I what?" Was the man daft? Why would he be paying any attention to Garrick when Genvieve was standing right in front of him, her lips so prettily pursed, ready to receive his kiss. He reached out to her and was surprised when she took a step backward.

"What's wrong?"

Instead of answering him, she shook her head at him. "I need to speak with you privately."

He sensed something was wrong and needed to be corrected. She was still in pain, but not complaining. His mouth lifted on one side in a crooked smile, marveling at her fortitude. She'd make a grand Highland lass.

"A missive just arrived, milord," a young servant announced walking toward them.

Augustin started to rise, but the young servant motioned to MacInness. "For milord MacInness."

His gut clenched—no one but Garrick and his men knew that he couldn't read.

Augustin nodded. "It could be from Annaliese."

Genvieve jolted at her mother's name, and he noticed that what little color she had drained from her face.

Pride be damned, he called out, "Garrick, read the missive for me. Genvieve, ye need to trust me, lass."

Huge gray eyes searched MacInness's face, but he didn't wish to explain now. Bloody hell, she was his wife, and she would trust him. He almost said as much, but she started to sway. He had her securely wrapped in his arms a moment later.

"Come, lass, ye need to be in bed." He cursed the fact that he *needed* to make love to his wife, but she was injured and needed to heal first.

"MacInness, wait," Garrick said.

He paused in the open doorway, urging Genvieve to rest her head on his shoulder. The fit of the woman in his arms was driving him to distraction, and wreaking havoc with his control.

"Whatever it is can wait, me wife needs to rest."

Garrick looked at him and nodded. "I'll send Jillian to sit with her."

MacInness was going to refuse the offer, insisting he would be the one to sit with his wife, but a hint of urgency in the other man's eyes stopped him. "Aye."

"Winslow," Genvieve whispered as he strode out of the hall. "I can walk."

He brushed his lips to her forehead and said, "I know ye can, lass," and walked up the stairs. "But I canna risk hurtin' ye," he added, walking in through the open door. "Besides, I've a powerful need to hold ye, and ye feel like heaven in me arms."

⇶⇷

HER INSIDES POSITIVELY melted with her husband's declaration. It wasn't one of love, but it was one of the need they both shared.

He set her on the bed and started to back away from her. "Winslow," she rasped, reaching out for him. "Please, don't leave yet."

"Lass," he sighed. "Ye're killin' me."

"I was afraid I'd lost you," she confessed. "Why didn't you tell me you were leaving?"

"Ye weren't there to tell."

"You could have left me a message."

"I didna trust anyone to give it to ye."

"You could have written one."

He stared at her for so long she wondered if he was going to answer her at all. "Nay, lass. I couldna."

She swung her legs closer to the edge and started to slide off. Winslow stopped her. "I wouldna move just yet."

"Why?"

"Ye need to rest," he said, looking at her as if she'd lost her mind. "And ye canna rest if ye're on yer feet!" He threw his hands up in the air and stalked toward the door.

"I need to hold you," she said. The need to be stripped bare and held against her husband's broad, brawny body had her blood heating and her belly fluttering.

"Nay, lass," he said, watching her expression change from worry to desire. "I wilna hurt ye further."

"I don't care if I use my hands or my mouth, but I have to touch you." She slid off the bed and slowly walked over to where he stood with his back against the closed door.

His amber eyes widened a heartbeat before the fires of lust ignited, and he pushed away from the door, walking toward her.

Their bodies met three paces later. His was taut as a bowstring, but she didn't care. He was going to give in, and she was going to make it memorable. She grabbed hold of his shirt and tugged at it.

"This has to go." She pulled it free from where he'd wrapped his kilt around it.

"Aye," he groaned.

While he watched, she reached down, grabbed the hem of his shirt, and yanked it up and off in one smooth movement, leaving his heavily muscled chest bare.

She licked her lips.

He moaned.

Before he could change his mind, she closed the gap between them and pressed her lips against his heart. But she wanted a true taste of him, so she flicked her tongue against the rock-hard pectoral muscles that taunted her with their beauty.

He shivered.

She moved her mouth over to the right, latching on to his nipple, and sucked for all she was worth.

"Lass, I canna—"

"Oh, I think you can," she whispered as she moved to his other nipple, running her hands up and down his spine, then dipping lower to cup and knead the taut muscles of his buttocks.

Heaven.

"Your turn." He pressed her hard against him and lifted her so the core of her womanhood pulsed against his shaft.

"Winslow…" she moaned, then wrapped her legs around his waist and locked them behind him.

"Ye'll have no one to blame but yerself for fannin' the flames, lass." He rubbed against her until she moaned. "I'll try not to hurt ye."

He walked over to the bed and laid her on it, not letting her unwrap her legs from around him. Gently, carefully, he stripped her out of her clothes and pressed his mouth to her heart.

She thought she'd died when he dipped his head just a little to the side and sucked her breast into his mouth. The pain in her ribs as he put more of his weight on her faded as his clever tongue and lips played with first one breast and then the other.

Genvieve was mindless by the time he'd removed his belt and let his kilt fall to the floor. His shaft sprang to attention, but he didn't give her time to admire the length and breadth of him. He locked gazes with her and slid home.

Her muscles tightened around him, urging him to go deeper still, until she felt him nudging her womb.

"Lass, I canna hold out…"

She lifted her lips for his kiss. "Then don't."

Her words triggered his release. As the warmth of his seed filled her, she stroked his back, kneaded his backside, and then ran her hands up into his shaggy red hair.

"I love the feel of you," he rasped against her heart.

"And I love—" Her breath was cut short as he shifted, and she saw stars.

"Genvieve, lass!"

Her world slowly came back into focus. Winslow's worried frown changed to one of outrage. "I told ye I'd hurt ye," he ground out, his body vibrating with anger.

She reached up and traced the line of his jaw with her fingertips. "'Tis my own fault, love—I needed to feel you deep inside of me."

Tears welled up, and she blinked them away.

"Dinna greet, lass."

"I'm not crying," she insisted as more tears welled up.

"Ye could have fooled me."

"They're happy tears." She sniffed them back.

"Oh, aye." He chuckled. "And I'm the King of England." Wrapping his arms around her, he rolled until he was underneath and she on top.

She was deliriously in love with the man shooting daggers at her as he cupped her bottom in his hands, kneading her flesh until she wriggled against him. Impossibly, he pulsed inside of her, growing harder by the moment until she felt her passage grow wet with need.

Unaccustomed to the position, she tried to move with him, against him, but need was overwhelming her ability to reason, and she floundered.

Winslow took the matter out of her hands as he pinned her to him with the flat of his hand and rolled them over once again.

He slowly pulled partway out of her, and she ached with the loss. He leaned his forehead against hers and whispered, "I didna think I could love ye more than the day I first saw ye, fightin' tooth and nail against those bastards," he confessed, sliding back inside of her until he was snug up against her womb, his weight pinning her to the bed. "But I do, lass. I'd no' be whole without ye."

"Winslow," she sobbed, "I—"

"Genvieve?" Lady Jillian called, knocking on the chamber door. "Are you all right?"

Looking up into her husband's amber gaze and seeing everything she felt for him reflected back at her, Genvieve smiled. "Aye, Jillian."

"Garrick said that you—" Jillian began opening the door, shrieked, then slammed it shut.

"I didna think the sight of me arse would have that effect on a female," MacInness said, chuckling.

"She's not woman enough for the likes of you, husband." Genvieve grabbed said arse in both hands, bending her knees and drawing her feet back until they touched her bottom, spreading her legs as wide as they could go, taking Winslow as deep as she could.

When he was so deep, she would swear he touched her heart. He began to pump, slowly at first, until the walls of her passage tightened around him. He picked up the pace until he was thrusting hard and fast, mindless to everything except pleasing her and searching for the release just within their grasp.

Her release slammed into her, triggering his. He came inside of her, the heat of his seed warming her from the inside out.

"Well now, 'tis glad I am that I'm mon enough for the likes of ye, lass."

Genvieve held him close and sighed. Contentment filled her as the musky scent of their lovemaking surrounded them, lulling her to sleep.

"I love ye, lass," Winslow whispered against her ear.

"Mmm."

Just as she was drifting off, something poked her awake. Exhausted, she grumbled, "What?"

"Ye didna give me the words back, lass."

"Words? What words?"

His eyes were hot with temper. "Dinna tell me ye take them back already?"

Awake, she knew immediately what he wanted and gave it to him. "I love you, Winslow MacInness."

"*Och*, well, I knew that, lass."

"Then why did you wake me up?"

"I needed to hear ye give me the words." He pressed his lips to her forehead. "Sleep," he ordered her.

And she did.

Chapter Twenty

"Do you think she'll ever get over the sight of me *arse*?" McInness didn't want to admit that he was embarrassed by the thought.

Genvieve giggled, snuggling closer. "I wouldn't."

He planted a smacking kiss on the top of her head. "But I'm yer husband, and it's right that ye've seen me bare-*arsed*."

"True." She rubbed her toes lightly up and down the back of his calf, driving him to distraction.

"Ye'll need to stop now, lass."

"Hmmm?" she purred.

Purred, just like a cat! MacInness couldn't believe it. "Yer ribs are tender and if they haven't broken clean through yet, another bout of lovemaking and they will." Just the thought of her ribs fracturing and spearing one of her lungs had him mad with worry.

She laughed—again!

"'Tisn't funny."

"Oh, aye." She laughed harder. "It is."

Capturing her questing hands in one of his, he held tight, bringing her hands to his heart. "I wilna be responsible when you're lying in bed a fortnight because ye didn't listen to yer husband, lass."

That finally got her attention. "Two weeks?"

He nodded, and at the worried expression on her face relented. "But if ye're good and do everythin' I tell ye…"

Her eyes went round with wonder. "Everything?"

His words backfired, and he imagined her pleasuring him with her mouth as he'd taught her. He fought the rising need unfurling within him. He had to speak to Garrick, remembering that's what the man intended earlier when he sent his wife up to sit with Genvieve.

MacInness pressed a chaste kiss to her forehead, the tip of her nose and first one eye, then the other. "Sleep, lass."

"I'm not sleepy." She closed her eyes.

"Good then, it won't take much to wake ye when I return."

MacInness hoped whatever Garrick had to say wouldn't take long. As he slipped from the bed, he looked back at the flushed woman lying amidst the rumpled linens. Her sooty lashes lay against her pale cheeks, tinged with color from their loving. His gut knotted as he realized he'd never loved a woman the way he loved Genvieve—and he'd never give her up!

Bending down, he retrieved his plaid and quickly folded the pleats, securing them with his belt. Tossing the extra length over his heart, he took one last look at his sleeping wife and went to answer Garrick's summons.

⇶⇶

"WHAT KEPT YOU?" Garrick demanded.

"The lass needed to relax and wasna cooperatin'."

The other man chuckled. "She reminds me of Jillian."

MacInness nodded as he walked over to the brazier and sat on the bench next to Garrick. "Tell me what happened."

Garrick nodded and relayed the events leading up to and including the attack. When he was finished, MacInness did the same.

"Did ye notice how similar the attacks were?"

"Aye. Did you recognize any of the men?"

"Nay." MacInness paused, then rose to his feet. "But you mentioned that my wife did."

"Apparently, there were twins involved, Jean and Claude," Garrick began.

"I'll kill the bastards." Augustin de Chauret boomed from the doorway to the hall. He stalked over to where they stood.

"Too late," Garrick reminded him. "They're both already dead."

"Where did she know them from?" MacInness asked.

The older man sighed deeply, then folded his arms across his chest. "My uncle's wife."

"Genvieve's mother?"

He nodded. "They were part of her personal guard."

"Do you know of any reason why Lady Annaliese would want to see her daughter dead?" MacInness hated the way the question sounded, but he had had to ask it. He had to know what Augustin knew about his uncle's wife.

"Up until she lost her babe five years ago, Lady Annaliese was both loving and giving."

MacInness looked pointedly at Garrick. "Did Genvieve have anythin' to do with her mother losin' the babe?"

De Chauret shook his head. "I don't know much about that time, mayhap we should be asking Genvieve," he said. "She was there when Annaliese lost the babe."

"She's restin' now, but I can ask the lass later." MacInness inclined his head, spun on his heel, and left the hall by the side door. Walking down the steps, he followed the path through the herb gardens, hoping to find Garrick's lady wife.

She was on her hands and knees pulling weeds from the neat little groupings of herbs.

"Lady Jillian," he called out.

She turned and smiled.

MacInness asked. "I've somethin' I need to ask ye."

She brushed her hands, and pushed to her feet. When he

offered his arm, she took it.

"If a woman wanted to rid herself of a babe," he asked, "is there a way to do so, without makin' it look like she did?"

"Aye," she answered, "with the right blend of herbs."

MacInness had thought so, but to have it confirmed eased one of the knots in his gut. "I'll need to be askin' the lass about her mother."

Jillian's expression was one of regret. "You don't think her mother did anything to miscarry a babe, do you?"

"According to de Chauret, Lady Annaliese was a changed woman after she lost a babe about five years ago."

"Why do you think she had anything to do with it?"

"I dinna know, just a feelin'." And he wished he had more to go on. Proof would help if they needed to stand against Genvieve's mother and father.

"I can ask Lady Eyreka if she knows the exact mixture," Jillian offered.

MacInness paused and looked down at her. "I canna ask Genvieve," he said. "She's lost two babes of her own and it still hurts her to speak of it."

Jillian's eyes filled with tears. "I couldn't imagine the pain she must have suffered, losing one, let alone two."

"Can ye think of a reason why a woman would want to rid herself of a babe?" He couldn't, but he'd never had to gain weight, drag his overburdened body through the daily chores, and then there was the birthing ...

"Only one," Jillian whispered.

When she looked up at him, MacInness instinctively knew what she was thinking. "Rape."

"How do we find out?"

Jillian shrugged. "We ask."

"What if she lies?"

"We ask someone close to her."

"Her husband?"

"If it's rape, there is a possibility it was her husband, but from what I've gleaned from Genvieve, they were happy in their marriage," Jillian said slowly.

MacInness's jaw tightened. "Aye. It *maun* be someone else, but who do we ask?"

"Her maid servant."

"Thank ye." MacInness escorted her to the hall and left her with Garrick. "I've a task to see to," he told the other man. "Will ye watch over Genvieve while I'm away?"

Garrick took his wife's hands in his. "I'll be right back."

She drew in a deep breath and looked resigned. "You two don't want me to know what you are going to do."

They looked at her and nodded in unison. "Fine, then," she said, walking out of the hall without looking back.

"I'm goin' to London," MacInness announced.

"Take Patrick, Eamon, and a small company of men with you."

He agreed, then asked, "Do you think de Chauret would let a few of his men accompany me on the journey?"

"For his cousin's husband?" Garrick asked.

MacInness nodded.

"Aye," Garrick said without hesitation.

"Where is he?"

"De Chauret's training with Henri in the bailey."

MacInness found the man and made his request. Within the hour, MacInness and a mixed company of what was left of his Irish Contingent and a few of de Chauret's Norman warriors rode out of Merewood Keep, headed for London and the truth.

⇶✖⇷

"D<small>ID MY HUSBAND</small> say when he'd return?" Genvieve couldn't believe that he'd left without saying goodbye…again!

"Nay."

She wondered why Jillian wouldn't look her in the eye and

reasoned that the other woman knew something Genvieve didn't. Something of import that involved Winslow.

Though her heart felt as if it were being squeezed of every drop of blood, every ounce of strength, she had to ask, "Is he meeting another woman, then?"

"Winslow?" Jillian sounded horrified. "Nay."

"Then what?" Genvieve demanded, rounding on her with her hands on her hips.

"Walk with me," Jillian bade her to follow along to the back of the herb garden.

Looking over her shoulder, Genvieve didn't see or hear a soul. "Tell me."

"I don't know of any way to ask without hurting you."

"Best just say it then," Genvieve urged, biting the inside of her lip so she did not interrupt again.

"Did your mother regret losing her babe?"

The question had all of the air whooshing out of Genvieve's lungs. When she could gather herself back together, she shook her head. "No."

"Did you find that odd?" Jillian asked pointedly.

"Aye," Genvieve answered. "As I'd been married for a short time myself and was looking forward to babes of my own."

"Did you notice a change in her after the loss?"

Genvieve remembered the black depression her mother had fallen into after losing the babe. "Aye. She was despondent."

"Did anything cheer her?"

Genvieve nodded. "The idea of going back to Normandy."

"When did she?"

"We didn't. Father was stationed here as part of the king's council, and my mother as an attendant to the queen."

"Did she speak of going back?"

Genvieve's mouth felt suddenly dry. "Every day."

"But your father, surely he would have tried to go home if it would mean so much to your mother."

Genvieve shrugged. "Theirs is a marriage of convenience that never grew beyond that convenience, though I know they shared happy moments."

"I see."

"I didn't as a child, but after being married to Francois, I grew to understand."

"About the babe," Jillian began, then hesitated. "I'm sorry, but there is no delicate way to ask."

"I know you are only trying to help me, so just ask me. I won't be offended."

Jillian hesitated, then blurted out, "Is there a chance that your father did not sire it?"

Genvieve's gut reaction was to say no, but something held her back. A conversation she'd overheard came back to her. There was a very good chance he was not the father.

"Aye," she rasped. "But I don't know if he is aware of that."

"What would he do if he found out?" Jillian pressed.

"He wouldn't lash out in a jealous rage," Genvieve said. "If that's what you mean."

The other woman nodded. "If he discovered something had happened at the time that was not your mother's fault, would he do something about it now?"

Genvieve thought about it, then took the other woman's hands in her own. "Just say what is on your mind, Jillian."

"Was your mother raped?"

Genvieve started to shake her head, then paused. "I don't know. I mean, I don't think so." She squeezed Jillian's hands and let go. "How would I know?"

Jillian started walking back toward the hall. "If she didn't want you to know, you wouldn't."

Genvieve wondered. "Mayhap there is a way to find out."

"I believe that is what your husband went to London in search of."

"A rapist?"

Jillian shook her head. "Answers."

"Why didn't he ask me?"

"Would you have had all of the answers he sought?"

Genvieve knew she wouldn't have and shook her head. "He still could have left me a note, or something."

Jillian shook her head. "He can't read."

The truth hit her like a blow. "Why didn't he tell me?" she whispered.

Jillian's look was incredulous. "Surely you've noticed that Winslow MacInness is a proud man."

Genvieve nodded. It all made sense now, the hesitation on her husband's part to answer her questions when she prodded him for an answer.

"You won't think less of him, will you?" Jillian's worry showed on her face.

"I may be hardheaded, but I'm not stupid," Genvieve said. "I love my husband. Whether or not he can read matters not to me."

Jillian looked relieved.

"I can read for the both of us…or I can teach him."

"His mother tried," Jillian said slowly.

"How is it that you know so much about my husband?" Flickers of jealousy slithered through Genvieve's belly.

"At one time, he was my only friend," Jillian whispered. "We talked of anything and everything, and then when my husband—"

Genvieve held out a hand in supplication. "Don't stop now, please."

Jillian cleared her throat and said, "When I thought my husband was going to set me aside, Winslow was there to listen."

"I have to ask," Genvieve said. "Did he do more than listen?"

Jillian shook her head. "He kissed me, but I told him I loved Garrick."

"And you still do," her husband said, surprising both women as he walked over to where they stood.

Jillian's smile blossomed from within. "Aye, husband," she said rising to her toes to place a swift kiss on his cheek. "I still do."

Garrick winked at Genvieve and swept his wife in an ardent

embrace. When the kiss seemed to go on forever, Genvieve realized she wasn't needed and retired to her chamber.

She'd need to rest. She had much to discuss with her husband when he returned.

A FORTNIGHT LATER, Winslow returned, but their party had increased in size.

"Mother?" Genvieve couldn't believe her eyes. Her mother had not set foot outside of London since their arrival, except for one trip north, but that had been seven years ago.

Had Jillian somehow guessed the truth? Had her mother been raped on that one journey north? The timing was right, but something about her mother's silence didn't feel right. Genvieve would just have to ask her mother.

While Lady Eyreka was settling Genvieve's mother into the solar, she went in search of her husband, finding him amidst the uproar in the bailey.

"And I say that ye lied," she heard him shout.

"Winslow?"

He turned when she called his name. "Lass, what are ye doin' here?"

"I wasn't about to wait for you at Sedgeworth, when I knew you'd return here first." When he made no move in her direction, she walked over to him and wrapped her arms around his waist.

He started to squeeze her, then stopped. "Are yer ribs healed, lass?"

She stood on her tiptoes and brushed her lips across his chin. "Oh, aye," she rasped.

He hesitated before sliding his arms around her back and lifting her in the air, twirling in a circle. "'Tis cause for celebration…later, wife."

She tilted her head back and laughed. When his lips met hers, she held on tight and kissed Winslow back with all of the pent-up desire she'd been feeling. He responded by kissing her breathless. When she sagged against him, he lifted her in his arms and turned to de Chauret. "The poor lass missed me. I've got to soothe her tender feelings."

Patrick's sharp bark of laughter echoed behind them as Winslow strode to the steps leading into the hall. Not pausing to greet anyone, he took the stairs two at a time. When they were behind closed doors, Genevieve whispered, "You take my breath away."

"I'll give it back to ye," he said before covering her lips with his.

"I missed you, husband."

"Ye'd best be showin' me how much, then, lass."

The gleam in his eyes had her belly fluttering in anticipation. "I don't know if we have time," she told him. "We're expected for a feast."

"*Och*, lass," he said, removing his belt and letting his plaid drop to the floor. "There's always time for lovin'—'tis how ye use the time that counts." He lifted her up and onto his erect shaft.

"Oh…I…" Words were beyond her as her husband walked over to the wall and leaned her against it, thrusting home again and again.

She shot to her peak and over before he'd broken a sweat.

"Aye, that's it, love," he urged. "But ye can take more of me." He lifted her off, carrying her over to the bed. When she would have lain down on her back, he stopped her. "Do ye trust me, lass?"

She lifted her hand to his face. "You know I do."

"Then let me love ye from behind."

"I don't think… That is, I don't know. I mean—"

"*Och*, ye've never been loved deep, then, lass."

"I don't understand."

"Trust me to teach ye." Winslow showed her how to kneel on the bed. When he knelt behind her, she tensed, but he rubbed his hands on her breasts and started to build the anticipation. When his fingers caressed her heat, she spread her legs a little wider to allow him better access. He let his hand rest on her womanhood and then tilted her at an angle and slid into her welcoming warmth, deeper than he had before, deeper than she'd thought possible. Her passage clenched around him.

"Winslow!" she urged him on, and he sank all the way inside of her, gloved in her tight, hot, wet heat. The fit was exquisite, the feeling decadent. And then he started moving, slowly at first, and then faster. She matched his pace, until he thrust in one last time and she screamed his name. He shouted hers. Instead of pulling out, he eased them onto their sides and held tight.

If she'd thought it possible, she would have prayed for their loving to produce a babe, one with red hair, freckles, and beautiful eyes the color of amber. But God had other plans for her. She'd already lost two babes, and didn't think she could stand to lose another.

While Winslow nuzzled her ear with his lips, he splayed a hand across her belly, possessively, protectively. Did he want children? Would he change his mind and be sorry she was barren?

"Whatever has ye stiffenin' up on me after cryin' out me name so they heard us in the great hall isna worth the worry."

"But—" she began.

He held her close. "I'm listenin', lass."

"It's nothing."

Winslow sighed. "Powerful bit o' nothin'."

Needing to distract him, not wanting to discuss her inability to have children, she asked, "So your mother is fine, then?"

Winslow kissed the top of her head. "Aye. I'm not sure who sent the missive, but the messenger was dressed in my clan's plaid."

"But the missive wasn't from your family?"

"Nay. 'Twas all a lie."

"I'm glad." And she truly was. Her husband's family ties were strong, though he was far from home.

"Now, lass," Winslow began, "about that little bit o' nothin' earlier—"

The knock on the door had them both reaching for the covers. He pulled them up and called out, "What is it?"

"Milady ordered bathwater for your lordship," a deep voice called out.

"Just a moment," Winslow answered, sliding out of bed. He reached for his plaid and fashioned the pleats once more.

Rather than wait for her to join him, he carried her bliaut and chainse to her and helped her dress, insisting she remain on the bed. "Dinna move, lass," he said. "I like the look of ye sittin' there, all soft and warm from our loving."

She blushed, and he grinned.

"Come in," he called out.

While the servants filled the wooden tub they'd brought with them, Winslow sat next to Genvieve on the bed, unable to take his eyes off her, watching her with desire swirling in the depths of his gorgeous amber eyes.

"If ye keep on lookin' at me like that, lass, we'll no' make it downstairs."

Genvieve laughed, but waited until the servants had filled the tub and left before remarking, "You must be exhausted. Let me bathe you."

"Ye can join me," he offered.

She laughed. "If I do, we will not make it downstairs in time for the evening meal."

"'Tis obvious ye didna miss me as much as I missed ye, lass," he said, stepping out of his kilt and into the tub.

He eyed her like she was the last sweet on an empty table. "Are ye sure ye won't join me, lass?" His gruff request and gleaming eyes had her changing her mind and reaching for the hem of her gown to remove it.

A short while later, more water was on the floor than in the tub, and the lovers finally got down to the business of washing.

"I never knew a bath could be so invigoratin', lass."

She blushed. "I'm sorry. I don't know what came over me." Genvieve couldn't believe the way she'd attacked her husband again. It was as if she couldn't get enough of him.

He bit her shoulder, and she moaned. "I don't think I could

possibly—"

"*Och*, lass," he whispered. "I know for a fact that ye can."

"We'll miss supper."

He gently lifted her, settling her onto his shaft. She tilted her head back and groaned. "I'm not hungry anymore."

"Ye will be." Winslow shifted and drove into her.

A LONG WHILE later, snug and dry, wrapped in her husband's arms, Genvieve drifted off to sleep, secure in the fact that Winslow had missed her and that he loved her. While relieved that she hadn't had to tell him about the bone-deep fear she held tight in her heart, she still worried that he would grow to hate her because she was barren.

"Sleep sweet, lass," Winslow whispered as he pressed his lips to her temple.

Chapter Twenty-One

"I still don't understand why she couldn't come downstairs to greet me last night," Lady Annaliese said to her husband and his nephew.

Augustin grinned. "They are newly married." As if that explained it all—and it did as far as he was concerned—he let the matter drop, changing the subject to the weather, their crops, and his own wife.

Lady Eyreka entered the room smiling, Jillian walking on one side of her and MacInness and Genvieve on her other side.

"Maman!" Genvieve rushed over to where her mother sat and would have hugged her, had her mother not moved out of the way.

"Annaliese," Aimory de Chauret warned, rising to his feet. When Genvieve would have stood quietly by, he stepped forward, enveloping her in his embrace. "I've missed you, daughter."

"Hmmph." Her mother looked away.

⋙⋘

She didn't know what she'd done to deserve such a reaction from her own mother, but sensed it had to do with not attending the welcome feast last evening. Looking up at her husband, she knew she'd make the same choice, given another chance. His touch was a healing balm she desperately needed.

He lifted their joined hands to his lips and kissed the back of her hand.

"You look well, Genvieve," her father said with a nod in Winslow's direction. "I knew you would be the right choice as husband for our daughter."

"He would never have been my choice," Annaliese ground out.

"Maman!" Shocked to the core, and embarrassed, Genvieve tugged on Winslow's arm to get him moving. Once they were seated, she leaned close. "Something's wrong with my mother."

Winslow mumbled something under his breath that sounded a lot like bitch. When she looked at him, waiting for him to repeat what he just said, he shrugged then smiled at her. He wouldn't use such foul language referring to her mother, would he?

Once everyone was seated, he leaned close and offered her a bite from their shared trencher. She smiled and opened her mouth. The bit of honeyed bread melted on her tongue. She licked her lips and watched Winslow's eyes widen, then darken with desire. It felt wonderful to be able to elicit such a strong reaction from her husband. Especially when she felt the same way.

He continued to feed her and halfway through the meal, her mother shot to her feet, crying, "Enough!"

Genvieve had no idea what was wrong with her mother, but something must be bothering her. "Maman," she began, "is something wrong?"

"You can sit there and let that barbarian touch you, and yet you ask me if something is wrong?" her mother bit out, acid dripping from her words.

Winslow pushed to his feet, but Genvieve laid a hand on his forearm, and he paused. "But he's my husband," Genvieve said, confused by her mother's outburst, hurting for the man she'd grown to love.

"In the eyes of God and man," Winslow added, resuming his seat after the insult he'd been dealt.

"You don't have to touch him in front of everyone, do you?" her mother asked.

Genvieve felt the flush staining her cheeks. She was embarrassed, but she would stand her ground. "I enjoy touching him, Maman," she said loud enough to be heard at the back of the hall.

Her mother's gasp of outrage was only slightly louder than Winslow's sign of contentment. "Ye have a way with words, lass," he said putting his arm around her and bringing her close enough to press his lips to hers.

"Aimory," Annaliese shouted, "do something!"

"What would you have me do?" he asked, not rising to his feet, though his wife was still standing.

"Bring her back to London with us and then to Normandy."

"We're not going back to Normandy," Aimory said slowly. "But you've known that for years."

Her mother's eyes began to dart from side to side and she started shaking. "I cannot stay here, Aimory."

Genvieve went to her mother. "Maman, please," she begged. "Come sit and have something to eat, you'll feel better."

"I will never feel better." Annaliese rasped. "Nothing can repair the damage that has been done."

"What are you talking about?" Genvieve asked, but her mother pulled away from her. "If you'd trust in Father, like I've learned to trust in Winslow," she said, "all would be well."

"I'll not have you suffer as I have," her mother screamed. "You'll not have to feel the brutal fists on your face and accept a rutting beast into your body as I have!"

"Annaliese, no!" Her father leapt toward her mother while Genvieve watched in horror.

Her mother's words had rendered Genvieve, and half of the people gathered in the hall, motionless.

Proof of her mother's horror seeped into Genvieve's soul. The hurt her mother had endured contorted the older woman's face as she reached for the eating dagger still hanging from her belt.

"Lassie, dinna move," Winslow shouted. He jumped to his feet and threw himself in front of the blade flying toward Genvieve. She jerked back to reality in time to see her mother's eating dagger bury itself deep in her husband's shoulder.

The sight of the blade sticking out her husband's body, with blood oozing down the front of his sleeve, turned her stomach upside down. But the screeching sound her mother made as she dove forward to claw at Winslow brought Genvieve up short.

"Maman ... no!" She stepped in front of her husband to stop her mother. When that did not deter her, Genvieve curled her hand into a fist and delivered a solid jab to her mother's jaw. Her mother went down like a stone.

She turned to her husband and gasped as Winslow pulled the dagger free. Tugging the threads loose from her sleeve, she balled the material up, and pressed it against the open wound where the dagger had been moments before.

"Ye'd best see to your wife," Winslow said to Genvieve's father, swaying slightly from the ugly wound.

All at once the hall was alive with movement and sound as Genvieve's father bent to lift his unconscious wife into his arms. The uproar died down a bit when he turned toward Genvieve. With tears in his eyes, her father rasped, "I am at fault. If I had hunted down the dog who raped your mother, none of this would have happened." He paused. "Can you ever forgive me?"

"If not for what Maman had tried to do to protect me, I'd never have met Winslow." Turning toward her husband, she let go of the tears she'd tried to hold back. "I'm so sorry. I never would have let her near you if I had any idea how she felt." Tears streamed down her face. "Forgive me?"

"Ye did a fine job, plantin' yer fist to her jaw, lassie," he rasped, brushing her tears with the tips of his fingers. "I'll make a

Highlander out of ye yet."

Genvieve smiled through her tears.

While her mother was carried out of the hall, bits and pieces of the past came together. "Jillian must be right," she whispered so only Winslow could hear her. "I cannot think of any other reason why she would try to kill you."

"'Tis the truth, everyone loves us, lass," Patrick said with a grin.

"Us?" she asked, feeling as if she'd come into the middle of a conversation.

"'Tis a long story, wife," Winslow said, watching her as she pressed against his wound.

"Can you not be serious?" she demanded. Lord, his blood was everywhere. "Lady Jillian, please help me."

"You're doing a fine job," Kelly said, walking over to where she stood maintaining pressure on her husband's wound. "I'll heat my blade, and we'll let Lady Eyreka sew him back together. She has a fine hand with stitches."

Genvieve couldn't speak, anguish swept through her at the thought of her mother trying to kill her husband. "Why?" she asked. "Why didn't she tell someone?"

Just then her father reentered the hall and walked toward her. "She came to me and explained what had happened, but I didn't react the way she expected. I didn't hunt the man down and kill him as she demanded."

He paused and nodded toward Winslow. "I discovered that she paid someone to deliver the message to you that your mother was dead. I am beyond sorry."

Genvieve watched the play of emotions flickering across her husband's handsome face. "Ye did what ye thought was right at the time." Winslow paused, then added, "I would ha' reacted a bit differently."

He cupped her cheek tenderly, while he said, "I would ha' hunted the mon down like a dog," Winslow bit out.

"And?" Garrick asked, as if he sensed there would be more.

"Then I'd skin him alive," the Scotsman said with no inflection in his voice.

Genvieve swayed, but kept her hands firmly pressed to his wound.

"Are ye all right, lass?" he asked tenderly, brushing the wisp of hair out of her eyes.

Fresh tears welled up and spilled over. "She hurt you," Genvieve cried.

"I'll mend," he promised.

Epilogue

Twilight was her favorite time of day. Standing atop the curtain wall with her husband at her side, Genvieve would carry their daughter, while Winslow carried their son. The guard would still make their sweep of the wall, but they'd slow their steps and lower their voices if the twins were sleeping.

"Moira's growing so quickly," Genvieve whispered, brushing a midnight curl off their daughter's forehead so she could press her lips there.

"Jamie's still bigger," Winslow boasted, reaching for his daughter, while Genvieve passed her off and waited for her husband to put their son in her arms. She brushed a flyaway strand of bright red off his cheek and pressed her lips to the spray of freckles at his temple.

"Did you ever think we'd have such beautiful children?" The wonder of it filled her still.

"Aye," he answered. "'Tis because I prayed for ye, lass."

Confused, she looked up into his beloved face and waited for him to continue.

"Ah, lass," Winslow said pulling her close and holding her against his side. "'Tis a family ye needed, so I asked God for a miracle."

"But I thought I was barren," she rasped, still not believing she'd been able to carry the babes to term and safely deliver them.

"Ye hadna been with a Highlander then, lass." Winslow winked at her and kissed her full on the mouth in front of the passing guard and their sleeping children.

"And that makes all the difference?" she asked, not quite believing him, needing to tease him. "Then why did you pray?"

"If we only had one chance, I wanted a son and a daughter," he said simply drawing his family against his broad shoulders.

"Ah, lass," he rasped. "Life is good."

"I love you, Winslow," Genvieve said closing her eyes.

"I know," he said grinning.

She shook her head at him. "Winslow!"

He sighed deeply. "You'd force me to say the words, then, lass?"

"Yes," she said waiting, and smiling.

"I love ye, lass."

She sighed deeply, "I know."

About the Author

If we have not met yet, I'm delighted to meet you. Here's a little bit about me...

I have been writing romance novels for almost half my life, well at least for the last 30 years. I'm a diehard romantic and have to confess the broad shoulders and wicked glint in the brilliant green eyes of a stranger had my breath snagging in my breast, my heart beating madly, and my future flashing before my eyes. At the age of seventeen, I'd met the man I knew I was going to spend the rest of my life with.

I write Historical & Contemporary Romance featuring characters that I know so well: hardheaded heroes and feisty heroines! They rarely listen to me and in fact, I think they enjoy messing with my plans for them. Over the years I have learned to listen to them! I have always used family names in my books and love adding bits and pieces of my ancestors and ancestry in them, too! Visit my website to learn more about my books.

Sláinte!
CH

C.H.'s Social Media Links:
Website: www.chadmirand.com
Amazon: amazon.com/stores/C.-H.-Admirand/author/B001JPBUMC
BookBub: bookbub.com/authors/c-h-admirand
Facebook Author Page: facebook.com/CHAdmirandAuthor
GoodReads: goodreads.com/author/show/212657.C_H_Admirand
Dragonblade Publishing: dragonbladepublishing.com/team/c-h-admirand
Instagram: instagram.com/c.h.admirand
Youtube: youtube.com/channel/UCRSXBeqEY52VV3mHdtg5fXw

Milton Keynes UK
Ingram Content Group UK Ltd.
UKHW021825311024
450535UK00010B/216